CINDERS & SALT

ECHOES OF VENTLIGHT BOOK 1

CAMERON O'CONNELL

ARGENTO
PUBLISHING

Cameron O'Connell

Cinders & Salt

Echoes of Ventlight Book 1

ISBN: 978-1-947709-45-4

© 2021, Cameron O'Connell / Argento Publishing, LLC

info@argentopublishing.com

To my mother, who encouraged me to explore new worlds when the real one simply would not do.

To my father, who drew whatever I asked him to no matter how ridiculous or far-fetched.

You both mean more to me than I can say.

A.D. XII KAL. APR. MMCDLIII A.U.C.

APRIL 1ST, 1770

Carcer on the Outskirts of Cappadocia

Temet nosce.

Know thyself

THE OLD PURIFIER

AND THE SEA

I

TO WHOM IT MAY CONCERN

*H*ow should one begin the last letter they shall ever write? Surely I am not the first to pose the question. Indeed, I wager there is a precedent for those whose heads are destined to part ways with their necks —some trite salutation, perhaps, addressed to whomever is most likely to give a damn. A cheery hail-fellow-well-met from the murderer in the third cell on the left.

A guilty man would, I expect, take the opportunity to tidy up after himself—to apologise to the loved ones of his victims or beg the forgiveness of disapproving, finger-wagging relatives. As I seek no clemency and have no family to disappoint, however, I suppose all I have left is this: my true and honest account of the cocked-up circumstances which led to this igno-minious and, frankly, rather anticlimactic end.

I do not relish the task. Scribing is a skill I learned late in life and have seldom practiced at length even before a homunculus tore into the liga-ments of my left hand. Not that penmanship is my concern. To the untrained eye, the cipher I am required to use appears little more than a jumbled mess of squiggles and lines—the sort a child might make if left alone with pen and parchment.

To tell the truth, my greatest fear is that I will not do the tale justice. Or, worse still, that I will not be believed. For Caesar's sake, I can hardly credit the events of the last few weeks myself, and I was bloody well there. There when the Phrygian king's curse took root and the damned proclaimed war on the living—there when the closest thing to a friend I ever had breathed his last.

But I am getting ahead of myself.

As I cannot be sure when or in what sorry state these missives will arrive, I suppose I should begin by telling you who and where I am. That way, if nothing else, one of our own can recover my corpse.

My name is Valentine IX. I am a Londiner by birth—a Barbari, to use the common parlance for those of us who were never wholly welcomed into the bosom of the Empire, but one step removed from those subjugated peoples known as slaves. Sadly, this distinction is lost to the natives of Cappadocia, many of whom equate one foreigner with another regardless of pedigree or creed—a reality quite literally beaten into me during the first of several unprovoked thrashings I endured at the hands of local inmates.

At first, I assumed it had something to do with my pale complexion and conspicuously Britannian accent. Or perhaps my matte black mop of hair which—despite its dull, unobtrusive colour—holds neither curl nor wave. By the time I realised it was all of these things and more, however, I had at least two shattered ribs, a cracked tooth, and bruises piled atop each other like too much paint applied to a ruddy canvas.

Were it not for the unforeseen sympathy of my jailers, in fact, I expect I would have already paid the price incurred by those bright-eyed invaders who once razed these lands—men with whom I share very little and like even less.

Since then, I have been transferred to one of several solitary cells in a remote cave on the outskirts of the city—what the natives call a *carcer*, I believe. I have also been given as much parchment as I could want and treated with a consideration bordering on dignity, neither of which I can account for except to say they must have discovered who or, at the very least, what, I am.

Of course, I will be sentenced all the same. Indeed, I imagine those slated to pass judgment upon me will share the sentiments of those prisoners who blackened my eyes and bloodied my stools, no matter my profession, while those qualified to speak on my behalf are either already dead or only too glad to see me suffer the same fate. Frankly, it is only a matter of time before the manner of my execution is decided.

What will it be, I wonder? Am I to be dragged to the gallows and beheaded, or possibly stoned to death in the center of town? Perhaps they will avoid the fuss altogether and have me poisoned in my cell. That, at least, would be a fate to look forward to.

No matter. I refuse to wallow in self-pity, regardless of the outcome. The Order's infamous library has more than enough maudlin memoirs cluttering its shelves without the lamentations of Valentine IX. I can picture them even now: whole rows stuffed with similarly truncated volumes, each suffering from correspondingly morose conclusions. Pathetic.

And yet, perhaps that is the point. Perhaps our unvarnished renditions of this mad world, authored by the men and women who watched it burn until they themselves were reduced to ash, remind us we do not suffer alone, or in vain. That—though we may never be properly recognised—we will never be entirely forgotten, either.

So be it.

As I have little else to occupy my time before a cold cook claims my corpse and the priests bicker over the rest, I shall start with this: I have committed many crimes, but of this one I am not guilty. The Habsburg girl is dead, her body so mutilated it will have been shipped to Vienna in pieces —that much is true. But I am telling you now the tragedy of her passing is not a sin I intend to add to my already considerable tally.

To list them all, of course, would take far more time and far more ink than I have been given. As one might expect, the total has grown exponentially since I saw naked flame brandished for the first time. I was a mere eleven years old, then—a foolish child whose finest trait was his refusal to be eaten alive. Indeed, I was charged with a crime that night, too, though the penalty for slaughtering what amounted to livestock pales in comparison to that of butchering a Praetor's betrothed in cold blood a mere week before she was to be wed.

But I seem to have jumped ahead once again.

Very well. If this is truly to be the last letter I shall ever write, then I suppose I should begin where my story began.

On the streets of Londinium.

II

THE BUTCHER & THE COLD COOK

*I*n those days I had no family, extended or otherwise. I had lost my mum to a fever that had cooked her from the inside some two years prior, my dad to the sea before I was born. Or so I had been told. My mum avoided that subject almost as vigorously as she avoided men in general, when she was not whoring.

Ironically, it was the physicians who pawed at her like any other tosser and then had the audacity to charge for the privilege who repulsed her most of all. A Khannish silk trader explained that word to me—irony. Now, all it reminds me of is my poor mum passed out in a pool of her own sweat because she would rather die than let any man take back from her that which she had rightfully earned.

Some might call that a tragic beginning, but then what street urchin's tale was ever a happy one that was not concocted out of thin air by some deranged romantic throwing words like *benefactor* and *inheritance* about as though we were all but one serendipitous encounter away from salvation? None that I ever met, of that much I can assure you.

And there were so very many of us back then, especially after the failed rebellion—hordes of living, breathing reminders of what happens when the soldiers never come home to claim what they left behind, burdened to wear the faces of dead men until we, too, met our end. Back home, they have begun calling ours the foundling generation. Personally, I think that is giving themselves too much credit. We were never lost.

We were discarded.

In those days I ran with a gang of pickpockets and fetchers—boys around my age who had no one to take them in or care whether they lived or died. We worked for a cold cook named Signore Garza who owned the coffin house in our exceedingly dodgy part of town. The Nest, as everyone called it, was the most industrialised and most overpopulated of the city's seven boroughs—every marketplace clogged with the guts of mangled machinery, every thoroughfare thick with swarming bodies, the air choked with the stench of steam and mould and shit.

As a thief, I suppose I could not have asked for a better home.

Indeed, it was not such a bad life. By day, the lads and I scammed and schemed—too young to be proper scared of anything more than going to bed cold or hungry, and too old to hope for more. At night, for the reasonable price of a copper deni, the cold cook provided a warm meal and a wooden coffin. In time, that quota became part of our vernacular, a phrase we used when trading favours or laying bets, which began with the mandatory "give us a belly and box" and ended with some outrageous, lopsided request.

It would be decades before I learned Londinium's coffin houses were, in fact, legally responsible for sheltering the city's surplus population—an Imperial decree which spawned dozens of real estate investments by savvy, unscrupulous merchants hoping to harness the free labour we orphans represented. Merchants who then hired disreputable expatriates like Signore Garza to pursue their interests. It was a tidy business arrangement that saw Garza's pockets filled, the merchants' wealth sheltered, and our own needs soothed if not precisely satisfied.

Still, I cringe to think on those nights we were forced to listen to Garza's rose-tinted revisionist history lessons, knowing he would send us out into the cold if we refused. The old swindler fancied himself an imperialist, painting glowing pictures of Londinium as a city second only to Rome at its height, regaling us with secondhand accounts of the years leading up to the the revolt, of a golden age when the Pontifex still governed in the east and we Britannians believed ourselves an integral limb attached to the body of an empire upon which the sun would never set.

And we listened, because we could not afford to do otherwise. Of course, from where we sat—and by that I mean in coffins carved to accommodate the corpses of children—darkness had claimed our accursed island a bloody long time ago.

Forgive me for seeming bitter, still. More than a decade has passed since I last stepped foot on Britannian soil, and yet the wounds I received there feel as fresh today as they were when I left. I still wake to the smell of blood that is not there, my hand reaching for the crude knife I once kept tied around my belly, my body aching from having been folded into the tightest possible ball during the wee hours of the night—a habit a survivor of the streets never entirely outgrows.

Of course, it was much easier to hide back then. I was born small, you see. Half-cooked, my mum liked to say. What I lacked in size, however, I more than made up for in savagery—a fact many urchins did not fully appreciate until it was too late. At first, I was content to gnaw at their fingers, claw at their eyes, and tear chunks from their ears. But that only made them angry. So, I stole myself a suitable blade and began taking trophies. Digits, mostly, though I was not above stealing scraps of rancid meat and pawning them off as dismembered tongues.

Within a matter of weeks, I had earned both a reputation and a nickname—a sobriquet that has accompanied me, in one form or another, to this very day: Little Boy Butcher.

Though they meant to tease me, I think, I must confess I rather fancied the name, not to mention the notoriety that came with it; in my mind, the epithet was a hex of sorts—a curse not unlike those we laid upon the sprawling, faceless Empire that had stolen from us an entire generation of husbands, brothers, and fathers, or those obscene execrations we leveled at the oppressors who collected our taxes and imposed our curfews.

Indeed, even as a child it was clear to me that we Britannians only maligned that which we could not wound—that we targeted individuals whom we had the capacity to harangue but never to harm. Perhaps that was why I found the moniker so endearing: on some level, I knew they were scared of me. Of what I might do to them.

By them, of course, I mean those lads about my age. The elder urchins had other things to worry about, like getting off the streets lest they end up press ganged and sent to some foreign shore to die in the name of expansionism.

In Londinium, that meant toiling away in the Vents or enlisting with the dragoons fighting in the Hind, assuming they were fortunate enough to pass muster. I say fortunate only because the Auxiliaries were rumoured to pay well and had a halfway decent survival rate, whereas working the Vents was a toss-up between dying a slow, agonising death coughing up the blue blood caused by the chemicals used to treat the steam, and a viciously quick one being flayed to the bone by the pressurised contents of a burst pipe.

You know, even now, even after all the horrors and atrocities I have seen, I pity those poor bastards most. It pains me to think their names will never grace the pages of any book, much less the spines; we would run out of trees, first. What might they have become in a kinder time or place? A shame we shall never know. But then, as my predecessor so often liked to bellow when he was in his cups: *Tale est Imperium!*

Such is Empire.

III

INTERLUDE: BULLY

*J*n all the time I spent on the streets, I knew of only one lad to enlist with a regiment. We called him Bully, on account his real name was Billy and he was a right bastard who enjoyed testing his fists on fresh faces. Bully liked to claim it toughened us up, but no one ever thanked him for it. I certainly never did; not three days after the landlord had my mum's body carted away in a box, the gangly whorespawn had knocked out two of my milk teeth and bloodied my nose on a whim.

Looking back, it could not have been more than a matter of weeks after Bully shipped out that the rumours began—my personal favourite being the one in which he took a saber to the throat courtesy of some dark-skinned caravan raider who liked to feast on the brains of his decapitated victims, a peculiar fetish that went unsatisfied the day he cracked open Bully's pitifully empty skull.

Though I desperately wanted it to be, I cannot tell you whether any of it was true. Every story we Londiners ever told grew darker in the telling, relying almost exclusively on what you might call gallows humour—assuming you find the notion of men, women, and children twitching until they piss and shit themselves particularly amusing. All I know for certain is that those teeth took ages to grow back in and my nose never was entirely straight after that.

Still, I can see now that was how the feeders got away with it for as long as they did: we Londiners with our perverse jokes and idle gossip. Had we paid closer attention, had we focused a little more on what was going on in our own miserable boroughs than what was happening continents away, then perhaps we might have noticed the empty coffins where bright-eyed children had lain the night before. We might have wondered at the silent alleyways, the abandoned street corners, the sleepy bridges. And maybe, just maybe, we might have banded together before it was too late.

IV

HARD COIN FOR HARD TIMES

*CW*hen the disappearances began, many Londiners assumed one of our own had sold us out to the Bloodbacks; though they would deny it, the local constabulary were notorious for snatching up those who would not be missed and selling them for a tidy profit, albeit rarely in such quantities over so short a span.

Others speculated the Varangians were somehow involved, despite the fact no one had laid eyes on one since the Puppet King's failed coup some fifteen years before. I suppose it made for an entertaining story, if not an implausible one. But then those olive-skinned, blue-eyed mercenaries had committed so many atrocities during their brief tenure on our soil that we blamed them for every unsolved rape and murder this side of the Thames.

In any event, we knew there was no point taking chances; if someone really was out there snatching the city's undesirables off the street, we urchins were the lowest of hanging fruit. Signore Garza and his ilk might raise a stink, of course, once enough of us went missing that they felt it in their purses. But that would hardly help those who were already gone.

As such, many of the lads began traveling in packs, avoiding their usual haunts lest they be rousted and sold off to the Reformatory of Sanctus Agatha—a glorified, government-funded work camp which prepared its inmates for life in the Vents. Or, worse, that they would be deemed mentally unfit and sent to where the real atrocities took place: the Sanitorium.

Initially founded to provide a haven for the deranged, the asylum had since become a den of depravity subsidised by donors who preferred the company of those who could not escape their perverse attentions. For some, that meant sex. For others, violence. Either way, everyone knew that if you were not broken by the time you went in, you would not have long to wait.

I had broken out of the Reformatory once already and had managed to avoid the Sanitorium altogether, though I would gladly have leapt from Boudica's Bridge before being sent to either. With that in mind, I traded the relative comfort of the coffin house for the unassuming rooftop I favoured whenever I could ill afford Garza's fee—a cozy crevice tucked between two chimneys that radiated so much heat I had to roll over every half hour lest I end up like a charred pig left unattended upon a spit.

Sadly, it was a temporary solution at best, and not just because I could barely withstand the scalding temperatures. At that height, the chemically-treated steam that wafted up from the undercity and drifted across the sky in mossy pockets seared the lungs and turned one's spit rancid within a matter of hours. I remember I spent three whole days and nights trapped above the eaves amidst those toxic clouds, once, fighting a fever that refused to break. And, though I survived, I will never forget the discoloured phlegm I hacked up over the next two months—the same blue gunk smeared across the mouths and chins of those miserable Venters destined to die clutching at their fluid-filled throats.

As such, I am sure you can imagine how eager I was to find proper shelter, and why I was so intrigued by talk of the Labour Baron. Having come to the Nest spouting some gentrified drivel about finding us deniless folk gainful employment, it seemed the man was offering would-be sailors an opportunity to join the crew of a merchant fleet headed to the Gallic States in exchange for three squares a day, a living wage, and a chance to get as far from Londinium as the ships could sail.

Initially, I admit I found the proposition hard to believe. You see, we Nesters were born grifters. We lied like we breathed and stole before we could talk. We cheated as though every toss of the bones would be our last. And those who lacked such talents? Well, they had no choice but to barter their bodies as labourers or whores—at least until they became old and haggard enough to sell their stories as beggars. Moreover, while one could blame these ignoble traits on necessity and circumstance, the fact remained that Nesters were perpetually on the lookout for a dishonest day's work.

Which meant the notion that any merchant worth their medallion would allow a single one of us aboard their precious vessel, let alone offer us a proper job, was absurd.

My reasoning faltered, however, when I learned the Baron was staking suitable candidates, offering an advance of hard coin, even to those whose cheeks would remain hairless for some years to come. I began to have visions of sailing across the Narrow Sea as a full-fledged member of a merchant crew, drinking my weight in Visigothian wine and filling my belly with Frankish cheese.

And yet, I remained skeptical.

After watching my mum die the way she had—not to mention surviving the streets of Londinium for several years—I knew enough about the world, about its cruelty and its inequities, to be cautious. I knew the Nest had earned its misleading appellation not because of the pipes and tubes which cluttered our streets and crawled over our homes, but because no one ever left. I knew the Baron's proposal had to be bollocks, just as I knew that the missing Londiners would never be seen or heard from again.

Of course, there was knowing, and then there was *knowing*—a distinction which lured me from my rooftop with its life-altering implications. Now, before you start questioning my poor judgment, know this: there is no desperation quite like that of a child who has very nearly starved or frozen to death.

You see, unlike the mild climes to the south, Londinium's cold snaps were, and indeed still are, notoriously perilous, especially for the inhabitants of the city's shabbier boroughs. Indeed, the previous spring's first thaw had exposed dozens of frostbitten corpses throughout our streets, their blackened, hoarfrosted husks littering the otherwise deserted thoroughfares like capsized boats in a sea of slush and muck. And so, with an early autumn creeping around the corner and a jacket so threadbare and undersized that I had split nearly every one of its seams, I could argue I needed every spare deni I could get my hands on—even if that coin came with unavoidable, nigh invisible strings.

THE BARON & THE AUREUS

he Labour Baron was a plump bastard with so large a gut that it threatened to pop the buttons of his ill-fitting frock coat. I despised him for it—sickened by his girth the way only someone who has spent sleepless nights curled around their hunger could be. Worse still was his gap-toothed smile and the soggy moustache which lay limp atop his upper lip; the Baron's tongue slithered out to moisten it through that gummy aperture when he thought nobody was looking, leaving the hairs slick and clumped like the matted fur of a wet dog.

Then again, I never had cared for his kind. As I saw it, the Barons were sycophantic blowhards, at best—glorified middlemen who represented the bottleneck between the unkempt masses and what few honest jobs there were, choosing who worked and where with all the discretion of a drunk taking swigs from unmarked bottles. At worst, they were shameless opportunists who traded favours and took coin under the table to supplement their already exorbitant incomes.

Not that I was fool enough to voice these opinions; such was the authority and influence of the guilds which employed the Barons that those who talked out of turn struggled not only to find work, but to stave off creditors and keep friends. Indeed, when dealing with a man such as him, one could either paint a fake smile across one's face, or a very real target would be painted on one's back.

The choice was yours.

The Baron watched me approach with a thin-lipped scowl, his gaze flicking disdainfully from my ragged clothes to my greasy hair and sallow cheeks. He hesitated only twice, taking particular note first of the sickle-shaped scar which still hangs beside my right eye like a crescent moon, then of the myriad, multicolored bruises speckled up and down my extremities.

When he spoke, it was with an affected, nasally intonation distinctly removed from the garbled Nester dialect I was used to. My childhood accent was a truncated, unrefined mess I had inherited from my mum's most frequent customers: dockhands who skipped over whole syllables like a whistlecoach weaving to avoid potholes in the street.

"Whatever foolishness you intend, boy, I suggest you forget this instant," he began. "I am not a man to be trifled with. Be on your way, or I shall call the city watch. And mind your hands when you go, assuming you wish to keep them."

"Oy, I'm no a thief," I lied.

The Baron's eyes narrowed.

"Word is you's got a job for us Nesters," I continued, my palms suddenly sweaty. "That so?"

"You want a job?" The Baron's laugh was like that of a braying horse. "You must be yanking my anchor, boy. Look at you. If you weigh five stone dripping wet, I would let you cut off my own arm and beat me to death with it. What possible use could you be to my employer?"

"So, you're sayin' there is a job, then?"

"Did you not hear what I just said?"

"I 'eard you. You said I 'av to be a fatty to do the job." I eyed the Baron's swollen belly and hawked a gob of spit onto the cobblestones, pleased to find it clear of the speckled blue gunk that had once saturated my saliva. "Can't see as 'ow that's fair."

"Do not be daft, child. I am saying you are not strong enough, and fair has nothing to do with it."

"What about the other lads you was just talkin' to, then?" I asked, jabbing my thumb in the direction the Baron's last recruit had gone a few minutes earlier.

"What about them?"

"Well, you told them where to go."

"And what's that got to do with you?"

"Everythin', Your Lordship. See these?" I pointed out the bruises purpling my arms and shins. "I got 'em wrestlin' those lads a few days back. Beat 'em all, I did. See, I'm tougher than I look, a'ight? Anythin' they can do, I can do better, I swear it."

"I am no Lord, boy," the Baron grumbled, though I could tell by the way he puffed out his chest that my intentional misuse of the title had pleased him.

The man appraised me a second time, his sopping wet lips pursed in thought. I straightened under his gaze, hoping he might think me older than I was; while I had grown several inches in the last year and might have passed for as old as fourteen in a pinch, I was as thin as I had ever been— little more than a flesh tent propped up by swelling bones that kept me awake more nights than I could count.

Indeed, I knew for a fact the Baron had little cause to hire me over my taller, stockier peers. Which was why I had hidden in the shadowed recesses of a nearby alleyway and watched him for half the day before making my approach, preparing the lie I knew I would have to tell if I wanted to stand even a chance of getting hired on. To this day, I do not know whether he saw right through my ridiculous tale about wrestling some boys I had never met while presenting bruises earned from clambering about Londinium's rooftops as irrefutable evidence to that fact.

All I know is that it worked.

"Why do I have the feeling I am going to regret this?" The Baron waved away my reply. "No need to speak, boy, that was a rhetorical question. I take it you are one of the orphan brats that inhabit this sorry place? No parents to track me down if you take the job and get yourself killed because you are too stupid to live?"

I nodded.

"Good. The Winedocks, tonight, eight o'clock. Do not be late, or the Royal Engineers will think you've come to rob them. And you would not want that, trust me."

"What about the advance, like the one you gave the other lad?" I asked, deciding to press my luck.

"Right." The Baron grunted and pressed a whole silver deni into the palm of my hand like it was nothing, though I equated its value instantly to a dozen nights in my very own coffin, at least. "If I find out you didn't show tonight, I will be coming back for that coin, boy. And I will take the interest out on your hide."

"And what am I to do, then? When I get there, I mean."

"I have no idea. The merchant I represent asked for extra hands. A lot of them." The Baron turned as if to leave, then seemed to think better of it. "Whatever else you do, see that you mind your tongue and avoid getting into trouble. Do as you are told, and my employer will see you sorted with thirty times what you have there in your hand."

I quickly did the math. "An aureus? You're 'avin me on!"

"I never lie about coin, boy." To prove his point, the Baron reached into the dainty pocket of his waistcoat from which he produced a solid gold piece pinched between his hairy fingers. "Whatever they ask of you, do it. Do it well, and perhaps they will groom you for a life at sea. The life of a sailor is always an adventure, or so they say. Should you cause any trouble, however...well, let us hope it does not come to that. For your sake."

I jerked a nod and left with the Baron's thinly veiled threat still ringing in my ears, careful to palm the coin I had been given in case anyone had been watching our little exchange. While my reputation for violence was enough to keep my fellow Nesters at bay, there were professional thieves throughout the seven boroughs who would leave you naked in the street under the very noses of the city watch—whose salaries their guild fees subsidised.

Fortunately, while still a great deal more than I had ever been willingly given, a silver deni was rather unlikely to attract that caliber of thief. A gold aureus, however, was another matter. With it, I could buy not only a new coat, but a whole wardrobe's worth of clothes. Indeed, I could rent out an entire room in a grungy dockside tavern for a month, if it came to that.

And so, come nightfall, I found myself heading towards the docks.

VI

THE PAINTED MAN

The Winedocks—a port so named for the peculiar shade of burgundy which stained both its waters and the hulls of passing ships—belonged to a ramshackle brigade of former Royal Engineers who had answered only to themselves ever since the fall of the regime that instituted them.

Though this meant that those who wished to dock paid dearly for the privilege, it was widely understood that this lopsided transaction came with a degree of discretion unknown to other such ports, and that the sanctioned ships with their vetted crews and legitimate cargo docked further south, towards the heart of Londinium, and therefore beneath the watchful eye of the Imperial gunships which routinely patrolled the lower Thames.

As such, I was not surprised to find the area all but deserted upon arrival. What did surprise me, however, was the unexpected appearance of the spectral figure who stepped out from the boathouse the instant I reached the waterfront.

The Royal Engineer's face was all but hidden beneath a white headscarf, the regalia of his obsolete uniform stained and tattered, its once rich scarlet colour now a muted shade of brown. He wore a broadsword on his hip, its basket hilt painted black, and carried a sailor's ventlamp with a dimmer and hand crank.

"The Labour Baron sent me," I called out, nervously.

The Engineer turned, unlocked the iron gate, and pointed towards the gaping doorway of a depot sitting on the river from which yellow-green ventlight spilled. Beyond it rose a two-masted frigate with furled sails, its squat silhouette visible against a backdrop of swirling steam painted silver by the light of the moon. I ducked my head and hurried past, disturbed by his eerie silence.

I need not have been; to this day, I have never heard an Engineer speak, not even to save themselves from certain death. Titus insists they cannot, claiming the Puppet King demanded their tongues be sacrificed to honour his short-lived reign—a testament to their loyalty. But then, Titus enjoys feeding me all manner of trivia that later turns out to be pure drivel, so please do not fault me if I am wrong about that.

In any case, within the warehouse several men moved crates from the dock to the ship's deck using a bulky crane while a bevy of hired hands bustled to and fro. Most of these were stout, muscled Afrikani clad in vibrant, patterned shirts draped over their silk trousers, their sinewy arms bare and glinting with sweat. Of the many Nesters I had expected to encounter, however, I found only a single beggar and a half-dozen lads, primarily those I had seen earlier that day, mucking about on the fringes of the activity.

I hovered in the shadows of the doorway, watching as the elderly Londiner circled the depot, painting each box with the eerie emerald glow of his ventlamp while the Afrikani prepared the crates for the crane's hook. The longer I lingered, however, the more I sensed something was amiss. For one thing, the Afrikani moved too methodically, too efficiently, to be mere hired hands—few do anything so well who have not done it dozens of times before. Of greater concern to me, however, was what had happened to all those extra hands the Baron had mentioned.

"Damn that swaggering shit, I thought I told him to stop sending children."

A square-jawed, thick-necked sailor with skin painted black with so many tattoos he seemed cut from the darkness itself came padding up from behind me with the bowlegged strut of a man used to walking on the balls of his feet. I danced away instinctively as he drew near, one hand pressed to the crude blade I kept sheathed beneath my shirt.

"Easy, now. There's no need for that. I just wanted to get a better look at you." The sailor tapped a left eye made of glass with one shockingly long fingernail. In his right hand he held a knife with a bright red apple spitted down its length, its juices dribbling off the blade. When he caught me staring, he held the fruit out. "Fancy a bite?"

I gulped and shook my head.

"Your loss."

The painted man put the apple to his lips and chomped down with relish, tearing free so large a chunk it seemed a miracle he did not slice open his own mouth or shatter teeth in the process. He studied me with his good eye as he chewed, the revolting sounds of mastication interrupted only by the occasional groan of the crank and the bellows of the men who worked it.

"So, what brings you here, little one?" he asked through a mouthful of pulp, his words predictably garbled. "Come to spy on us?"

I shook my head again, more adamantly this time.

"So the Baron sent you, then, did he? I'd wager he paid you in advance, too."

To this, I said nothing.

"Worried I'll try to have it off you? Smart lad. Oh, well. I guess it can't be helped." The sailor fetched something from a leather pouch hung round his neck and flicked it at me. "Half now, half when the night is through."

"What's this?" I asked, finding my voice at last as I inspected the unfamiliar coin. Featuring the weathered profiles of a woman and a bearded man, neither of whom I recognised. It was certainly not the aureus the Baron had promised, but instead some foreign coinage. Perhaps that mystifying currency they used on the other side of the ocean where, unlike the rest of the world, they had long ago rejected the trappings of Rome.

"It's a drachma. The coin we traders use. Less volatile exchange rates than the Imperial standard, if you gather my meaning."

I had no idea what he was talking about.

"Never 'eard of it." I tossed the coin back, oblivious to its value. "And neither 'as anyone else I know. I 'av to 'av coin I can spend. I want the aureus the Baron promised."

"If he promised you an aureus, he lied." The painted man swapped his foreign coin for two others. "I'll give you one silver deni now, and the other when the night is done. Take the deal, or give me back the advance and crawl back to the rat's nest you came from. Your choice."

I wavered for a moment before accepting the offer. Not because it was generous, but because I had no interest in handing over the silver I had already spent in my head. Besides, now that I knew the Baron was as full of shit as I had originally suspected, I began to see why there were so few of us; while a couple silvers for a night's work was hardly something to sniff at, no Nester worth their salt would waste hours earning that which they could steal in seconds.

"The Baron also said the Captain was lookin' to hire 'imself a crew," I added as an afterthought. "Was he lyin' about that, too?"

"The Capetan," the sailor corrected, holding his hand above mine for a long moment before dropping the silver onto my open palm. "And no, the Baron wasn't lying. We ship out in a few days. If you do well between now and then, maybe the Capetan will consider bringing you aboard. We could use a new cabin boy."

"Why, what 'appened to the last one?"

"He asked one too many stupid questions. Got his tongue ripped out and drowned in his own blood."

"Oh." I coughed into my fist to conceal my discomfort. "So, what am I to do, then?"

"It's simple. See those crates lined up portside? Go and check those ropes, especially the knots. Make sure they are good and tight. We can't afford any of those boxes coming loose once they've been hooked. Once you're done with that, check in with the big Afrikani, over there. His name's Ekon. He may have something special for someone your size."

"You want me to check knots? That's all?"

"Is that not enough for you?" The sailor raised his knife and eyed his apple as though plotting his next bite. "Maybe I should have you climb the rigging in the dark and scrub the masts clean, instead? Or maybe you'd prefer operating the crane, with all your hard-earned experience working heavy machinery?"

"I was only askin'," I mumbled, defensively.

"Well, from here on out, I suggest you keep your mouth shut and your hands busy. That is unless you want to end up floating down the Thames come sunrise."

With that, the painted man waved me off towards the open doorway. I closed my fingers over the cool metal in my hand, trying desperately to ignore that nagging sense of unease in the back of my mind and to remind myself that I had another just like it coming, provided I lasted the night. Of course, had I known how hard that would prove, I expect I would have run away screaming—coin be damned.

VII

THE EMPTY CRATE

*T*he Afrikani ignored me entirely as I went about my business. What few lads there were nearby perked up at my arrival, their expressions wavering between wariness and hostility, but I paid them little mind as I began working my way from one crate to the next, halfheartedly tugging on each knot I came to.

The sheer monotony of this task left me with plenty of time to fantasise about what might be found within these mysterious containers. Given the Winedock's dubious reputation, I strongly suspected contraband goods—the ivory tusks of the elephantis that roamed the Afrikani grasslands or the foul Khannish teas rumoured to grant otherworldly visions. Or perhaps something more volatile like wax-sealed pisspots filled with burnsand or glass vials packed with shards of ventstone.

Before I knew it, I had completed my task and found myself twenty paces from a darkened corner of the warehouse where a half dozen or so containers sat unattended. After a furtive look around, I slipped between two rows of stacked barrels barely wide enough to accommodate my budding shoulders, wishing I had thought to steal a ventlamp. This far from their verdant glow, all I could make out were rough shapes and indiscernible silhouettes.

When at last I reached the other side, I felt for the nearest container and fumbled with its sides, testing the integrity of its seams with my eager fingers and grimy nails—certain all I needed was to find one structural weakness, one loose nail or rotting board, to uncover a treasure beyond my wildest dreams.

I was doomed to fail, of course; the containers had been treated with water-resistant alloys and then soldered shut with alchemical agents that could only be removed using an antithetical compound. It was this precautionary measure, one of many the feeders employed to guarantee their cargo reached its destination no matter the circumstances, which ensured their wares survived all manner of catastrophes.

Though I could not have known any of that at the time, it did not take long before I drew back in frustration, my fingers stinging from countless futile attempts. I had just turned to leave, my imagination still running rampant with thoughts of baubles and munitions, when I noticed something odd: a neighbouring container—visible now that my eyes had finally adjusted to the gloom—had been pried open.

The wood was splintered along the entire length of the nearest seam, a series of haphazard, unsettling incisions marring that edge. I stepped closer, peering through the gaping hole it left behind with bated breath, itching with anticipation.

The crate was empty.

Clearly, whoever had been here before me had taken their treasure and run. I sighed and leaned back to study those strange incisions. The work of a crowbar or the claws of a hammer, perhaps? Except these widened where they should have tapered and got deeper as they receded into the empty box, which could mean only one thing.

The container had been opened from within.

As it was too dark to see how deep the gouges went, I thrust my arm through that aperture and ran my fingers along the wood, feeling for those furrows. There were more, I realised—dozens more, all layered atop each other like someone or something had been clawing at the walls. A chill ran up my spine as I caught a whiff of rank, rotted meat and—beneath it—the musty odour of mothcloth.

"And what do you think you're doing back here?"

Pulse racing, I whirled to find the painted man slipping between the barrels, slinking forward an inch at a time. The sailor's false eye glinted in the light of the ventlamp he carried, his face a cruel, ink-stained mask pitted with shadows and promising violence.

In that moment, I knew I had to make the choice all thieves make when caught red-handed: to run, or to lie.

"I noticed this 'ere box was open and went to check nothin' got pinched," I insisted, slapping the side of the container. "Wasn't nothin' inside when I got 'ere, though. Looks like whatever it was got pinched. A shame…"

The sailor froze, stiffening so violently that I could not be bothered to finish my sentence. He raised his ventlamp, staring wide-eyed at the empty crate, though the pupil of his left eye remained fixed in place amidst all that off-white paint, moored like a black ship on a shore of bones. Then—without so much as another word—he began scuttling backwards, shouting for the Afrikani he had pointed out to me earlier.

"Oy, what is it? What's the matter?" I cried, alarmed. When he did not reply, I hurried after him, catching up just as the Afrikani arrived.

"What is it, Capetan Moustakas?"

"Wait, did 'e say Capetan?" I interjected, tugging at the painted man's sleeve. "You lied to me!"

"So I did, now shut up!" the painted man hissed, swatting my hand away before turning to his ebony-skinned companion and speaking in a hushed whisper. "Ekon, I think one of the beasts got loose. Are all your people accounted for?"

Alarm pulled the Afrikani's face in multiple directions, tugging first at his thick lips before prying open his heavy-lidded eyes. Ekon spun in a slow circle, his gaze flicking from one man to the next as the work died down. The Nesters, who were considerably more attuned to such things than most, dropped what they were doing immediately and began creeping towards the exit. Sensing the wisdom in that, I thought to do the same when Ekon spoke again.

"Ode is gone." Ekon pinned a hand to either side of his mouth and called to his fellow Afrikani. "Has anyone seen Ode?!"

As if on cue, a harrowing scream erupted from the deepest recesses of the depot.

VIII

BAIT

*P*andemonium broke out as the few remaining Nesters fled the warehouse, streaking off into the night like startled cats. The Afrikani, meanwhile, huddled back-to-back in hastily arranged pairs. I had already turned to flee, myself, when I caught sight of the painted man—the ship's Capetan—drawing a serrated blade as long as my forearm from a sheath at the small of his back. Its quicksilver surface roiled like storm clouds, curling up and down its toothed edge in intricate circles. I froze, mesmerised by the sight of what I would one day call a Medici bonesaw.

Though rare, the Medici instruments—named for the family of ruthless merchants and politicians who requisitioned them from da Vinci himself— are a batch of surgical tools notorious for their ability to cauterise as they cut. Indeed, the decided advantages they offered surgeons made them a staple of modern medicine for nearly a century before the Medicis disavowed the Empire and sailed west to the Caesarean islands, taking their enormous wealth and the bulk of their trade secrets with them.

Since then, despite many attempts to reverse engineer their unique design, the mercurial properties of the alchemically-treated alloy had proven impossible to recreate, relegating those few that remained to mere novelties—priceless trinkets that occasionally changed hands on the black market, or were exchanged over the course of a back alley transaction.

I knew none of this at the time, of course. Indeed, the closest I had come to an operating table was the day the Reformatory nurse attempted to drive a spike through my eye and into my brain, the botching of which is to blame for the crescent-shaped scar which mars my cheek and brow. Still, I knew the blade's worth—recognising it the way you would the beauty of a woman or the value of a masterpiece. With it in hand, I could stroll into any shylock's shop and name my price.

I could be well and truly rich.

"There's only one of them," Moustakas told his companion. "Our investors won't be pleased about the loss of inventory, but they knew the risks. What we cannot afford right now is more bribes, which means we need to deal with this before the watch or one of those damned Engineers come poking around asking questions."

"Yes, Capetan. But shouldn't we try to save Ode, if there is only one beast free?"

"Ode is dead."

"But Capetan—"

"If he weren't, we would have heard more screams. Now, go bar the door. In fact, put one of your men on it. If anyone comes, tell them we had an accident. Better yet, tell them we had an infernite leak. That should keep them off our backs for a while."

"Yes, Capetan."

"When that's done, gather your best hunters and find me."

"Yes, Capetan."

Moustakas motioned with his lavish blade, and Ekon took off shouting in his native tongue. The Capetan turned and caught sight of me leering. "What are you still doing here?"

"I...well, you see—"

"Nevermind. It doesn't matter." Moustakas sheathed his blade, seized me by the hair with enough force to earn a startled cry, and began dragging me towards the sound of that scream. "Let's find a use for you, shall we?"

"Oy, let go! That 'urts!"

"Then stop struggling," Moustakas snapped. "I must say, you have the devil's own luck, boy. If you hadn't found that empty box when you did, we might all have ended up in the stocks by sunrise. I suppose I should be thanking you for that, but then you're the only one who didn't run."

Ekon returned with his fellow Afrikani while I snarled and thrashed like a dog caught by the tail. "Capetan? What are you doing with that boy?"

"Isn't it obvious? We need bait."

"But Capetan...he is just a child."

"Why, so he is!" Moustakas replied scornfully as he fended off my clumsy efforts to pry his hand away from my scalp.

"We agreed we would not hurt the children."

"No, we agreed we wouldn't use them as food."

"Capetan, I—"

"For Caesar's sake, this is our last shipment, Ekon! Three years! Seven ships in seven ports, six of which have already moved on. Do you really want to throw that all away?"

"Of course not, Capetan."

"Me either. Now, you and I both know there's only one way to draw their kind out into the open. So, unless you're offering to sacrifice one of your own people, I suggest we stop wasting time."

The Afrikani gazed down upon me with pity, but I could see in his eyes the Capetan's words had swayed him. I was on my own. Sensing it was now a matter of life and death, I fumbled under my shirt, took hold of my crude knife, and drew it free. I tried to drive it into the Capetan's side, to gut him and make a break for it, only to be stopped short by a massive hand latched around my wrist like an iron manacle.

Ekon yanked my arm back, wrenched the blade from my fingers, and barked a command in his native tongue. Three of his men gathered close in a tight formation, each armed with a spear as tall as I was. I continued to writhe and curse, howling obscenities at the top of my lungs until a vicious backhand connected with my skull. The blow nearly knocked me unconscious, and I tasted blood from a gash in my cheek.

"Take him," Moustakas insisted, passing me off to his larger companion as he inspected his stinging knuckles. "And see he keeps that mouth of his shut."

Ekon did as he was told, hefting my limp body and carrying me under one arm as though I weighed nothing. He and his fellow countrymen trailed the Capetan, headed towards the place where the scream had come from—a darkened corner where the refuse of every port could be found—passing corded baskets filled with indiscriminate detritus, spiraled mounds of waterlogged rope, and the shredded remnants of burlap sacks.

Just as I had begun to gather my jumbled wits, Moustakas snatched me back from the Afrikani, forced me to my knees, and yanked back one of my sleeves. He snapped his fingers, ignoring my pitiful attempts to pull away. "Pass me the knife you pulled off the boy."

"Yes, Capetan. Here."

Moustakas took hold of the knife and, with alarmingly practiced ease, slid the blade across the exposed meat of my forearm. I squealed in agony, clutching the injured arm to my chest the instant I was released. Though only a superficial cut, hot blood began to spill from the wound with startling rapidity, seeping through my shirt and staining my trousers. I huddled in on myself, struggling to overcome the sudden bout of nausea which gnawed at my gut.

"Would it not be less cruel to kill him first, like we did the others?" Ekon asked, his voice coming from what felt like dozens of paces away.

"Probably. But this isn't a feeding, and a fresh meal makes for better bait. You and your hunters should know that as well as anyone. Now, fan out! I can hear the thing coming."

The sudden anxiety in Moustakas' voice snapped me out of my momentary fugue. I swallowed back the bile threatening to spill into my mouth and strained my senses, desperate to know what was coming.

Something scraped across the floor, and one of the Afrikani adjusted his ventlamp to bathe that patch of warehouse in sickly green light. At first, I saw nothing but a pile of mouldy straw, a few cracked barrels strewn across the floor, and—further back—nebulous shadows draped across stacked pallets like dark sheets over unused furniture. Then, from out of that murky darkness, a genuine nightmare emerged.

IX

THE GHOUL & THE CAPETAN

*S*he shuffled into the light on all fours, so thin I could see the bones of her ribcage, the ridges of her bowed spine raised to form a row of tented flesh—her skin a pale, peaked colour utterly devoid of blood or blush, like that of a day old corpse. Hairless, noseless, and naked, she moved with the sinuous grace of an animal—pacing back and forth on her hands and feet like a predator, her sagging tits hanging limp like the teats of a pregnant dog. Her eyes glowed neon green, animated by the same infernal light that Ekon's men held trapped in their glass lanterns.

And yet, what held my attention most was the foul creature's lipless mouth and the flinty, petrified teeth which lay nestled within those grey gums like mould-riddled kernels clustered on a cob of rotted maize.

"Once it has the boy, pin it in place with your spears," Moustakas advised, hovering perhaps a couple paces away with his bonesaw in hand. "I'll do the rest. And remember, whatever you do, avoid the mouth. Ghouls can chew through damn near anything, even bone."

Ghouls. I experienced a shiver of recognition at the name. Though I had never before seen one, I had heard of such creatures. They were the monsters that devoured impious children—fiendish creatures that rose from unhallowed ground wearing the flesh of those who had refused to acknowledge the Almighty, cursed to wander for eternity in search of the nonbelievers whose profane blood they craved.

Or so the pontifices would have you believe, at any rate. In fact, according to them, you had but to reaffirm your belief in the Lord in the presence of a ghoul and you would be spared—an inconvenient and often fatal test of faith, to say the least.

The truth, of course, is far more complicated. In reality, ghouls are not so different from any other scavenger; they haunt cemeteries and church-yards, disrupting graves to gorge themselves on dead flesh and decaying bones like ravenous vultures. Indeed, they are only truly dangerous when they are underfed, or cornered.

This particular ghoul, unfortunately, was both.

As I watched, she scented the air through the gaping holes in her face, gnashed those cragged teeth, and stalked towards me like a dog with its hackles up. I was too terrified to do more than whimper, my heart lurching in my chest so violently I thought it might leap out of its own accord. Part of me wished it would do just that—at least then I would die quickly.

When the ghoul finally rocked back onto its heels to strike, however, some impulse—the very same which had prompted me to bite the thin-lipped nurse when she approached me with that barbaric metal rod—demanded I fight back.

That I do something, anything.

With a ferocity that belied my wounded arm and aching skull, I spun and launched myself at the unsuspecting Capetan, tackling him at the ankles just as he raised his blade. Moustakas barked out a yelp of surprise, pitching forward onto his hands and knees—one of which took me in the back, leaving me feeling hollow-boned and bleary-eyed. I cannot recall whether I cried out. Indeed, all I can remember is the terrified, blood curdling shriek Moustakas let out just before the ghoul struck.

A fount of hot blood cascaded across my back and side, warmer than any bath I had ever taken. I blinked away tears and glanced over one shoulder to find a grotesque face buried in the crook of the Capetan's neck.

I stared, transfixed and horrified, unable to look away even once she began gnawing her way up, her jaw clenching and unclenching with almost mechanical precision despite his every attempt to pry her loose. Eventually, the Capetan's screams became more and more distorted until—with a crunch reminiscent of a boot treading over shattered glass—they died out altogether, superseded by the abhorrent din of mastication.

Seized by a terror I cannot properly convey in words, I scuttled out from beneath the Capetan's corpse, only dimly aware of the various aches and pains which had been so all-consuming mere minutes ago. Once free of all that dead weight, I scrambled to my feet and found shelter behind a barrel.

After drawing several shaky breaths, I looked down to see I was coated in a sticky, vermillion patina—the bright scarlet of arterial blood intermingled with patches of darker, more venous liquids. Nearby, the Afrikani were engaged in heated conversation in their own language, gesturing madly to the ghoul and her meal. I could still hear her gulping down the Capetan's pulpy remains, and a quick glance revealed her curled around Moustakas' painted corpse like a neglected child, burying her face into the stub of his neck.

This time, when the nausea came, it won.

X

NAKED FLAMES

I groaned, wiped at the corner of my mouth with the cleaner of my two sleeves, and crawled away from the resulting pool of sick. And that is when I saw it: the Medici bonesaw, lying perhaps a dozen paces from where I sat. The priceless instrument must have fallen from the Capetan's hand, I realised, and gone skittering across the floor. I scurried forward heedlessly on my hands and knees until I at last knelt over the quicksilver blade.

It was lighter than I would have thought, the leather handle too bulky for my tiny hands. I turned it over, admiring its surreal sheen, and began to have visions of gold coins flowing over my hands like water—of warm baths and hot meals, of soft beds and hard liquor.

I rose, favouring my right side, and saw I had come up behind the ghoul without even realising it. She was on all fours, now, mounted over what was left of the body. Some distance beyond her stood the door—barred, of course, but still my best chance at escaping this nightmarish place. I began limping in that direction, the Medici blade naked in my hand.

To this day, I cannot tell you why I did what I did next. Perhaps it was the sheer revulsion I felt watching her consume a man whole—her swollen, distended belly lathered with blood. Or maybe it was something more primal than that—an instinct in the back of my mind like the one that urges us to step on spiders. Whatever the reason, when next the ghoul raised her chin to swallow all that gristle, I was in position and prepared to strike.

The blow was messy.

The saw-toothed blade jammed almost immediately, stuck fast in the meat of the ghoul's throat. My hand, numb from the jolt and weak from blood loss, slid right off the handle as she peeled away—a hissing sound trailing from her charred, steaming flesh. She began flinging herself about like a mad dog, rolling and leaping until at last she dislodged the blade, a sizzling wound left in its wake.

The ghoul clamped one hand over the gash and gnashed her grisly teeth, spinning in circles like a three-legged bitch chasing her tail, searching for threats. It did not take her long to spot me; I was too weak to run and too exhausted to hide. Indeed, when she came for me, I simply clamped my mouth shut, closed my eyes, and prayed for it to be over quickly.

My mouth was impossibly dry as I braced for the impending agony, my heartbeat pounding in my ears.

But it never came.

Instead, a startled yip—followed immediately by a cacophonous thud—brought me to my senses. I opened my eyes to find Ekon straddling the ghoul, hacking at the creature with the Medici instrument. She thrashed beneath him, bucking so forcefully it was as if the Afrikani weighed no more than a child hoping to secure a pig-a-back ride. He was flung aside and went skidding across the floor.

The ghoul, her flesh steaming from a dozen cuts, rolled to one side and had already begun to rise when the first spear took her in the shoulder. The next went through her thigh. Soon, three more joined them, each held by yet another Afrikani as they fought to keep her at bay. Meanwhile, Ekon had rejoined the fight. With every slash, every cut of the Medici blade, her convulsions weakened until—at last—she could do naught but twitch.

Ekon began sawing at her throat while the others looked on, the smell of rancid, burning meat saturating the air as he worked to sever the creature's head from her neck. For a moment, all was silent except for his laboured breathing and the steady rasp of the blade. Then, with a grunt of triumph, he staggered to his feet. His fellow Afrikani slowly gathered around, presumably to admire their companion's grisly trophy.

"It is done," one of them said in the common tongue. "Now, what are we to do?"

Before Ekon could reply, an acrid stench cut through the warehouse's briny odor, overwhelming even the robust bouquet of blood. A sudden wave of heat flared against my back, and I whirled to gawk at the frigate, shocked to discover it on fire—real fire, the kind that blazes bright orange and emits smoke instead of steam.

Though I had heard stories, I had never before seen its like. True flame had been outlawed centuries before I was born, of course—supplanted by the refined infernite which powers our society and bathes our cities with its verdant glow. And yet, from the very first I felt the allure of that crackling dance, fascinated by those forked tongues and the forbidden language they spoke.

Of course, in this particular case that dull roar was accompanied by the sound of ghouls being incinerated; trapped in their crates as the heat stripped them of flesh and bone, the scavengers cried out as one—a chilling chorus that reminded me rather forcefully of mewling cats.

Ekon and his fellow Afrikani raced to the dock's edge as one, shaking their fists at the smoke-laden sky. I, meanwhile, cradled my injured arm to my chest, aware of a lancing pain in my side that seemed to ebb and flow with every ragged breath I took.

I knew that I should run. Now that true flame was involved, the Blood-backs would have no choice but to storm the docks and arrest everyone in sight. There would be inquiries, no doubt. Executions, too.

And yet, I lingered in the glow of that blazing ship. Partly because I was far too tired to run, and partly because I had nowhere to run to. Between my injuries and the nose-rankling stench of smoke clinging to my blood-stained clothes, not even the coffin house was safe. Indeed, Garza would have happily buried me alive rather than risk being associated with an arsonist.

As I considered my increasingly diminishing options, I noticed a hooded figure silhouetted at the dock's edge holding a freshly doused torch—the rags at one end charred and smoldering. Even from a distance, I sensed his was a macabre presence, bearing the indelible mark of those perpetually steeped in blood. Of course, it is entirely possible I was imagining such things, for I knew what he was the instant I laid eyes upon the symbol stitched into the material of his cloak.

A Purifier.

An agent of Alexandria, tasked with eradicating the monsters that had plagued the world since the dawn of time—members of an Order so ancient and so arcane that their existence had become an oratory device, framing a bedtime story the same way one might say "before the first warship sailed to Carthage" or "when Londinium was but a riverbank and Rome a slew of seven hills."

What I did not know, however, was that I was looking at the man who would one day become my mentor. The man who would steal me away from the city of my birth. The man I never got the chance to properly mourn, and now likely never will.

Nero VIII.

May the Devil have mercy on his soul.

A.D. XI KAL. APR. MMCDLIII A.U.C.

APRIL 2ND, 1770

Carcer on the Outskirts of Cappadocia

Caveat emptor.

Buyer beware.

NERO AND THE GHOUL SHIP

VALENTINE'S REFLECTION

I

INTERLUDE: BREWING STORMS

When I awoke this morning, it was to an unusually gray day absent the sunlight that typically pierces the porous ceiling of my prison cell, though I doubt I would have noticed were it not for the odd behaviour of my neighbour, who—apart from a few isolated instances of sleep speak—has yet to utter a single word.

I can hear him pacing even now, his naked feet slapping rhythmically against the stone floor, his barely coherent ramblings punctuated by a single Greek word: *tempestas*. An odd choice. Once an appellation attributed to a fickle weather deity sacred to the Anatolians, the name has since become synonymous with the calamitous sandstorms known to ravage this other-worldly place. As such, I can only assume my fellow inmate is either incredibly pious or remarkably prescient.

Of course, I will know which soon enough, for when the *tempestas* begins, it does so with a whistling sound akin to that of a boiling kettle—a byproduct of violent winds gusting among the towering spires that rim the city. Next, the horizon will become saturated with rust and grit, painting the sky a surreal, scarlet hue that fades only once every surface is caked in ochre dirt. Stranger still are the forked tongues of claret-coloured lightning which arc across the sky while peals of thunder crack over and over again above one's head like a never-ending barrage of cannon fire.

Of course, strangest of all is how joyously the Cappadocians welcome it and the promise of wealth it brings.

At the first howl of those turbulent winds, they seek shelter in the subterranean labyrinth beneath the city only to emerge in huddled clusters to rove the rufescent landscape like survivors of some horrific battle. What little daylight hours remain they will spend sweeping the sediment into piles outside the local monasteries, at which point their priests use a famously proprietary alchemical process to create a terra-cotta lacquer with a hue prized by aesthetes throughout the Empire—customers including theologians from Antioch, Roman senators, and even Nubian kings.

As I write these words, however, there seems little cause for concern. The air remains stale and listless, the walls have not yet begun to sweat, and the turnkeys continue to banter conversationally in Greek as they play jack-bones with the pits of stone fruit imported from Constantinople.

Though I listen closely, I struggle to understand much of what they say. Like so many of those who came late to the Order, my linguistic capacity never extended far beyond my own tongue, just as my application of mathematics rarely ventured beyond the empirical, my comprehension of mechanics beyond the rudimentary, or my grasp of strategy beyond the crude.

I would love to blame my tutors for these deficiencies, but the truth is I was a mutinous adolescent who refused to learn that which had no immediate, practical value. Proof, perhaps, that the Order is right to deny admission to initiates of a certain age. But then, I had something their younger, more studious pupils lacked.

Ruthlessness.

Callousness.

Brutality.

Which, I suppose, brings me back to Nero.

The man is—was—a legend. Indeed, if this is the first the Order is hearing of his death, let me say this: he went out on his terms. And I would know; though unpleasant to admit, Nero was the closest thing I ever had to a friend—a grizzled, recalcitrant bastard who saved my life more times than I could count.

It was Nero who sought me out in the Londinium stocks that fateful night. He who bribed my jailers and who shipped me off to Alexandria with a hastily scribbled note of introduction. Indeed, it was Nero's words to me that day which inspired me to become something more than a grifter destined to die in the gutters of the only home he would ever know.

"What we do upsets people," Nero explained as we wandered the wharf in search of a ship bound for Alexandria. Foghorns blared beneath a drab sky and the taste of ash was heavy in the air. "Some say we're profiteers. Beneficiaries of a war that will never end."

The Purifier's voice was a brittle rasp, the mottled flesh of his throat so badly scarred it dribbled from chin to chest like melted candle wax. Armed as he was beneath his fur-trimmed overcoat, it was no surprise that furtive glances and hateful stares dogged our steps, though I must admit I found the polarised attention maddening.

"Others claim we're charlatans swindling the superstitious masses for everything they've got," he continued. "Then there are those who call us mercenaries. State-sponsored murderers who've risen too far above the law and should be put down like dogs."

"And you actually let 'em talk about you like that?"

"Why should I care what they say? By the time our services are required, those gibbering idiots are only too glad to pay for the privilege."

Nero paused to survey the Thames, his gaze lingering on the distant smoke still drifting off the charred remains of the Winedocks. The flames must have spread, I realised, consuming the warehouse as well as the ship before the city watch could get it under control.

"They're like children playing make-real, calling themselves heroes and us villains," Nero went on. "But just wait until one of their loved ones wanders into an alley arm-in-arm with one of those fanged devils, then see how they come running. Wait until the local farmers watch their crops die overnight, or the nobleman's son gets mauled by a beast with glowing eyes that refuses to die. That's when they turn to us. That's when they send for the Purifiers who have always stood between them and every foul thing they refuse to believe in until it has them by the throat."

"So it don't bother you to see 'em lookin' at you like that?"

"Why should it?"

"Because if t'weren't for you, they'd still be feedin' people to those things."

"Perhaps, but they don't know that. Nor will they."

"Huh? Why not?"

"Because we don't advertise our kills. Purifiers take credit only when we must, and the same is true for blame. Take that ship last night. Yes, I was able to sneak aboard and cause that fire, but what of those sorry bastards who died because I refused to act sooner?"

I frowned, struck by the ramifications of his question.

Nero shook his head. "They may call us Purifiers, but there's nothing pure about what we do. We tread in death's footsteps and leave a feast for crows in our wake. Make no mistake, child, this world is on fire. And those fools you call heroes? They're the ones trying to put out the flames."

"And what's that make you lot, then?"

"We're the bastards controlling the burn."

I I

INTERLUDE: THE JOB

The merchant brig Nero chartered on my behalf was meant to reach its destination in a matter of weeks, making port first in Hispania before passing through the Strait of Cadiz, resupplying in Cyprus, and sailing south to Alexandria. Enough time to get my sea legs, learn to tie a few knots, and pick up a bawdy shanty or two, at most.

Instead, it took nearly three years.

I spent the majority of that time aboard a frigate crewed by the very men who sank that merchant vessel—Thracian privateers, mostly, masquerading as diplomatic envoys. As their captive, I tended to their chickens, washed their clothes, and scrubbed their decks. In return, they taught me to read maps, to set bone and sew flesh, and to make grenadoes from burnsand, metal, and glass. I also picked up a few things on my own—like how to swim for my life, how to take a lash without blacking out, and how to kill without remorse.

All in all, it was a robust education.

I will admit it was not until the latter half of that third year, a few months after the first mate made the fatal mistake of confusing a naval galley for a pleasure barge, that I spared even a thought for Nero or his mysterious Order.

I had only just been released from a Syrian prison and sold to an Arabian sheik who had it in his mind to build a castrati choir like the one he had seen in Milan as a youth—a confession he made on the second night of our journey over a steaming bowl of meatballs he called *kofta*—when a company of Armenian bandits ambushed our caravan outside Babylon. I fled, finding refuge beyond the city walls. For the first time in years, I was free.

I was fourteen years old by the time I reached Alexandria and had long ago lost Nero's letter. Indeed, it would be over a decade before I again laid eyes on the man who had plucked me from my home and charged me with becoming a slayer of beasts. By then, I had already become a full-fledged Purifier with a fair number of kills to my newly acquired name—an arcane tradition which sees us all rechristened and enumerated with felicitous distinction.

But I sense I am losing the thread again.

Suffice it to say, I had every reason to bear a grudge against the man who never came looking for the orphan he cast out into the world like shark bait on a fishhook. Perhaps I would still, if not for the charge of malfeasance which landed me in front of the Order's Arbiters for a crime so heinous I dare not speak of it. That day, it was Nero alone who defended my actions, Nero who proposed our partnership.

In the four years that followed, Nero and I worked a couple dozen cases together—though none quite like this one. In fact, this was the sort of job Nero typically avoided, if only because it had everything he hated: a high profile employer, a dearth of hard evidence, and not a single corpse to speak of.

And yet, there we were, on a routine investigation into the suspicious activity surrounding an excavation site several miles outside Cappadocia—a fact-finding expedition funded by the excavation's patron, Archduke Joseph Benedictus II, heir to the declining Habsburg empire and, consequently, the elder brother of the girl I am accused of hacking to bits.

III

THE PRINCESS & THE STEWARD

A swift kick to the shin woke me from a fretful sleep, as it so often did whenever I drifted off in Nero's company. As a general rule, the sour-faced Purifier did not believe in sleep. I certainly never saw him do it. Today, however, it came as a surprise. We were not due to arrive until dusk, and the sunlight peeking through the skyship's hastily drawn curtain was bright enough to earn a hiss from yours truly.

"Stand ready, Valentine. The client's on board, and he wants to talk to us."

"On board?" I rubbed at my eyes and swung myself round to find the wily veteran looming over me like some immutable monument to stoicism and grit. When first we met, coarse grey strands had climbed the Purifier's temples and peppered his moustache, each unruly strand jutting out from beneath the beak of his nose like a wharf rat's whisker. Years later, his was a mottled, ravaged countenance—a puckered swarm of scars and creases swathed in stubble and capped in silver thatch.

"That's what I said," he replied.

"Since when does a client want to meet us?"

"Since today, apparently."

The bench groaned as I hunched forward, its blue velvet upholstery worn to a dull, flat sheen from overuse. A quick survey of the compartment by the light of day revealed a similarly shabby decor—exactly what one might expect of an economy cabin. Feeling more cramped than I had in the dark, I gestured Nero back, shooing him away as I would a dog. The senior Purifier shot me a withering look, retreated half a pace, and reached for the door. He spoke over the sudden thrum that permeated the air once he slid it open.

"Come and join us on the dining deck when you're ready. And clean yourself up. It's not every day you have tea with an Archduke."

I waited until the door slithered shut before retrieving the pinstriped cravat which signified my rank from the crank of a doused ventlamp, bemused to find its glossy amber surface smeared with stains that would never come out no matter how thoroughly I washed the bloody thing. I worked it back and forth over my knee to smooth out the worst of the wrinkles, sighed, and ducked through the flimsy door which led to the cabin's private lavatory, the luxury of which was mitigated by the fact that one had to straddle the toilet simply to wash one's hands. To my vexation, the mirror mounted on the wall was fashioned from the cloudy, canary yellow glass found exclusively beneath the shifting dunes of the Great Sand Sea—a testament to both the opulence of the Florentine flagship and the folly of those who equated style with substance.

As I fussed with the cravat and fiddled with the lapels of my double-breasted waistcoat, I studied myself in its filmy depths, unable to decide whether the amorphous reflection belonged to me or to some viscous sea creature. A proper looking glass would have revealed a haggard man in his early thirties, his gaunt face a sanctuary for shadows, sharp edges, and dark circles. I ran a hand through my sleep tousled hair, ensuring the unruly mop lay flat against my scalp, and sighed for a second time.

"That'll do, Valentine," I muttered, mocking Nero's gravelly pitch and the overtly condescending tone which more or less typified our relationship. Not for the first time, I found myself wondering how much longer it would take before the senior Purifier spoke to me as a colleague and not a subordinate. A few more years, perhaps? More likely a decade, I decided, assuming either of us lived that long. To be honest, I no longer cared one way or the other. Our partnership, no matter how lopsided it seemed at times, was quite possibly the only genuine connection either of us had left—and we knew it.

I left the lavatory and stepped out into the narrow corridor, eyeing the winding staircase which connected the ostentatious upper decks of Italia's latest gravity-defying contraption, and incidentally crossed paths with a harried steward toting a copper bucket brimming with shaved ice. We collided with startled cries, the metal pail clattering to the floor so raucously it could be heard even above the skyship's incessant drone. Indeed, the ill-fated accident drew immediate attention from the cabin at the end of the hall.

"What is going on out there?"

The voice belonged to a rosy-cheeked blonde who literally stuck her head out to check on the disturbance. She had a doughy face, its youthful chubbiness accentuated by the slight cleft in her narrow chin, an aquiline nose which hovered above a prim mouth, and a pair of glacial blue eyes that glittered the moment she realised what had happened.

"Signore, I must apologise!" The steward began dabbing at my jacket with a handkerchief as though his bucket had held a far less stable liquid, so flustered he did not even notice the girl leering at us from the cabin at the end of the corridor. That is until he caught sight of my face, at which point he jerked back and bowed. "Please, Signore, I do not want any trouble."

"It's fine," I muttered as I fetched his bucket from the floor. "There won't be any trouble. It was my fault for not looking both ways before leaving the room. Here, take this and go."

The steward retrieved his copper container, bowed a second time, and was moments from retreating when he saw we had an audience. The blonde had moved into the middle of her open doorway, beyond which I caught glimpses of a larger and far more lavish cabin than my own—though I expect it was the girl's attire and not the extravagance of her compartment which had diverted the steward's attention, for draped across her narrow shoulders was the pelt of some great beast, its flat, boneless face lying limp across her chest in such a way that her pale blue neckline peeked out through its gaping sockets, giving the fell creature the faintest illusion of life.

Upon further examination, I noticed that its fur had been fastidiously brushed—the result far more alluring, I imagined, than nature had intended. Indeed, I was fairly certain the skin belonged to that rare species of grey wolf native to the inhospitable regions north of the Iron Colonies. A dire wolf, they called it, capable of chasing down a racehorse at full gallop and gnawing off a man's leg with a single bite. The result was somehow both gaudy and barbaric, like a misshapen crown made entirely of jewels.

"Signorina, please forgive us," the steward said, his third bow so abrupt he very nearly fumbled the bucket a second time. "We did not wish to disturb you."

"Disturb me?" That flicker of amusement grew until the girl's smile was perhaps as wolfish as the trophy she wore around her neck. Now that I could hear her clearly, I realised she had a distinct Germani accent, albeit refined to such an extent that it was very nearly pleasant.

"Yes, Signorina."

The blonde waved the comment away with the casual arrogance of the privileged. "I am hardly disturbed, Herr Steward. Merely disappointed. I thought I might find a pleasant distraction waiting for me out here, but I can see now I was mistaken."

"A distraction, Signorina?"

"That is what I said, yes. Is my accent terribly difficult to understand? Perhaps I must work harder at my elocution lessons in the future."

The steward blanched. "Please, Signorina, that is not what I meant. I only hoped to point out there are a great many delights on board to keep the Signorina occupied, should she wish it. The observation deck on the top floor is a very popular choice. As is the vapor lounge on the *Ex Machina*'s port side, should you wish to partake in local custom. And of course there are the eateries on the first and second floors of the dining deck, where all manner of international delicacies may be found and enjoyed."

The steward took a deep breath as though to continue but was saved the trouble when the blonde began laughing, one hand held demurely over her mouth.

"You must forgive me, Herr Steward. I was only teasing you. Though I must admit I find your suggestions worth consideration. I will be sure to take them into account should I ever be allowed to wander freely. But please, I do not wish to be rude. Would you do me the honour of intro-ducing your companion?"

"I am afraid I cannot, Signorina." The steward glanced sidelong at me and gestured between the two of us. "The Signore and I are not acquainted. We simply ran into each other here in the hallway, as you can see."

"Then perhaps you would do me the courtesy of introducing yourself, mein Herr?" The girl tilted her head to one side in exaggerated fashion, and pressed a single digit to her lips—an affectation favoured by precocious children and crafty merchants alike. Indeed, the pose often meant the same thing: someone was about to get what they wanted.

"That is highly irregular, Signorina," the steward scolded. "I do not wish to intrude, but a young woman such as yourself should wait for—"

The blonde held up a hand. "You would do well not to finish that sentence, Herr Steward. What I do and to whom I speak is my business, and mine alone."

The steward choked out a response that could only loosely be dubbed an apology before turning to me, jutting his chin in her direction as though it was somehow my responsibility to counsel the young woman on the importance of propriety. When I did not, the steward huffed and planted himself firmly between the two of us as though we needed to be kept apart.

With a bemused sigh, I turned my attention to the girl herself, expecting to meet the mischievous gaze of a vain, spoiled child. Instead, I found desperation—the quiet sort one glimpses in the too-white eyes of a battered wife as she repeats the lies she has been instructed to tell, or the unhinged smile of an aging mistress who gave up everything for an unrequited, dwindling love.

The girl turned away, rubbing at her arms as though a draft had blown by, and I found myself itching to find and punish whomever or whatever had put so wretched an expression on so young a face. Unfortunately, stepping in to rescue strangers from the unhappy circumstances of their lives was neither my responsibility nor my prerogative. Indeed, were I to intervene every time I encountered someone who was suffering, I fear I would never have time to do anything else—especially my job.

"The steward is correct, Signorina," I said, at last. "I am afraid our introduction shall have to wait until a more appropriate opportunity presents itself, should such a time ever arrive. And, speaking of time, I seem to be running rather late. So, if you both will excuse me, I should be on my way."

Fortunately, neither the steward nor the girl attempted to detain me further—a fact for which I was grateful considering further delay was bound to earn me several more kicks to the shin over the coming days, and that assumed the ever-punctual Nero was feeling magnanimous. If not, well, let us just say that the coffin dodger had a remarkable flair for cruel and unusual deterrents.

One time, I watched him tether a defiant dockside worker to the rail of a departing ship while describing in meticulous detail the agony of being dragged along in the vessel's wake. Of being hounded by the beasts below with their jagged teeth and slimy tentacles. Of being pulled under again and again until one became so delirious with pain and exhaustion that death became a welcome respite. Unsurprisingly, by the time he cut the blubbering bastard loose, every sailor in earshot was willing to talk.

And that was Nero in a pleasant mood.

IV

SKYSHIPS & PETTY SQUABBLES

*T*he first-floor dining room was empty but for a few well-dressed passengers huddled over their gilded tea sets, sipping from trendy, tricoloured glasses shaped like tulips. This high up, the perpetual hiss of pistons was little more than a murmur—loud enough to ensure privacy, but hardly so raucous as to distract from the grandeur of the deck itself what with its floors of marbled cork, vaulted alabaster ceilings, and ostentatious table settings. Unfortunately for me, none of those magnificently prepared tables were occupied by Nero or our employer.

As I scanned the occupants a second time, another steward—this one dressed head to toe in assorted shades of cream—caught up to me.

"Signore," he whispered, "your companion asked that you attend him and the Archduke on the observation deck at your earliest convenience."

"Did he now?" I grimaced as the phantom weight of an imaginary tether cinched tight across my chest, leaving me wondering what it would feel like to be dragged behind a moving ship.

"Signore? Are you unwell?"

"Just grieving the loss of a good night's sleep. If I'm lucky. Did my companion say anything else?"

"No, Signore. Though I may have, how shall I put it...sanitised his request. His vocabulary was more colourful than one usually encounters aboard this vessel."

"That's putting it mildly." I sighed, "Oh well. So, the observation deck, you said? And how do I get there, exactly?"

"Go back the way you came, turn left at the staircase, and follow the signs to the skylift. Ask the operator to take you to the top floor."

"Won't that require a first-class ticket?"

"Ordinarily, yes. But, as the Archduke is a valued customer held in the highest possible esteem, you need not concern yourself with such trivialities. Word of your arrival has been sent to my colleagues above. May I be of any further assistance?"

"No, thank you. That should be all."

"Excellent. *Vale*, Signore."

"Cheers," I replied, preferring my native farewell to that of its Imperial counterpart.

As I turned to leave, I wondered whether I might use the change of venue to excuse my tardiness. The decks of a skyship were as notoriously difficult to navigate as its sides were to scale, after all—a reality imposed by their unique design.

If you have never before seen one with your own two eyes, I suggest you start by picturing a child's spinning top. Indeed, with their swollen frames and narrow tips, the external specifications of the gyroscopic aircraft routinely mirror those of their architect's most beloved toy—a testament both to da Vinci's brilliance as well as his droll sense of humour.

Not that there is anything remotely whimsical about the gargantuan machines; the hulking behemoths drift through the clouds like overturned mountains, their cast shadows creeping so slowly across the landscape that their pilots have to change course every few months lest the crops in their wake suffer from insufficient light.

Aside from this, they have little in common. Some are coated in metallic paint and draped in reflective material so that they blaze brighter than the noonday sun, while others remain utterly bereft of pomp, their pewter exteriors dotting the horizon like errant ink blots.

Their interiors, likewise, could not be more disparate. Glamorous leisure vessels like the *Deus Ex Machina*, for example, are meant to cater to the needs of their passengers as they coast from one major skyport to the next, whereas their economical cousins have long ago swapped sleeping quarters and observation decks for sequential seating and recessed windows. And yet, despite all its flaws, sky travel has grown increasingly popular among peerage and peasants alike.

Of course, it was my contention then as well as now that the bloody things are floating death traps destined to one day descend upon our cities like lumbering meteors and wipe out civilization as we know it. But then I suppose I have a healthier respect for gravity than most. In any event, all thoughts of excusing my delinquency were disregarded by the time I caught up to Nero on the observation deck.

It seemed now was not the time.

"Because that is just not what we do, Archduke," Nero growled under his breath.

Nero spotted me from the corner of his eye and gave a terse shake of his head, but it was too late. The Archduke, whose back was to me, swung about and fixed me with a surprisingly level gaze. I expected him to be angry the way most aristocrats would be when told anything other than what they wished to hear. But instead, he smiled, revealing uncommonly straight teeth and a cheery disposition that very nearly reached his eyes.

Having never met the man, I was surprised to find the Archduke an exceptionally pasty, long-limbed fellow whose livery—most notably his jet-black long coat with its cuffs and collar dyed Imperial red—served only to exacerbate the flush of his ruddy cheeks, cleft chin, and bulbous nose.

"Ah, Herr Valentine," the Archduke said with a dip of his head, his crisp Germani accent shockingly familiar. "You must forgive me for dispensing with the social niceties, but I was moments away from defending the ratio-nale behind my unusual request."

"The answer will not change, Archduke," Nero assured him. "We are not childminders."

"I do not believe I said you were, Herr Nero."

"There is no forgiveness necessary, Your Grace," I interjected in a clumsy attempt to diffuse the growing tension. "It's entirely my fault for arriving late. Though, may I ask, is there a relation of yours onboard? A young, blonde woman, perhaps?"

"My sister, Maria Antonia." The Archduke pursed his lips, his roseate complexion taking on even more colour until the pale flesh around his eyes and his chalky forehead stood out like a court jester's half mask. "If she has left her rooms against my instructions, I should attend to her. This conver-sation shall have to wait."

"Oh, no, Your Grace," I replied, hurriedly. "The young lady was still in her cabin when I last saw her."

Despite our similar heights, the Archduke looked down his nose at me, his gaze heavy-lidded and vaguely threatening. "Do you mean to say you spoke with my soon-to-be betrothed sister in her private chambers without a chaperone present?"

"Surely that's not what he meant, Archduke." Nero shot me an eloquent look. "Is it, Valentine?"

"Not at all. I spoke to her from the hallway, Your Grace. I had an unintended dust up with a steward in the corridor, and the noise must have caught her attention. My apologies. I did not intend to disrupt your conversation, only to comment on the uncanny resemblance between the Archduchess and yourself."

"I see." The Archduke let out a long sigh, coughed out a laugh, and clapped my shoulder the way one might a drinking companion. "Then there is nothing to apologise for. In fact, I believe this only strengthens my case. Can you not appreciate my dilemma, Herr Nero?"

"I can, and I do, Archduke. But my position stands. Purifiers make for poor nursemaids."

"It is fortunate that my sister does not need a nursemaid, then. What she needs is protection. Until her betrothal is secured and my family's legacy guaranteed, her safety is my main priority, and I simply cannot be in two places at once as I will be needed elsewhere."

"The job you hired us to do is—"

"Yes, so you have said. But please understand, Herr Nero, I will gladly pay extra for—"

"Enough!" Nero barked. "We are not whores, Archduke, to be used how you see fit."

Nero's stern rebuke thundered throughout the observation deck, earning disbelieving stares from all those within earshot. Indeed, the Emperor himself would have thought twice before snapping at an Archduke, especially in front of witnesses. Despite their declining influence, the Habsburgs had ties to the Imperial bloodline that went back generations— bonds which afforded them both a great deal of respect and a healthy dose of fear.

And yet, thanks to the labyrinthine charters drawn up many centuries ago between our Order and the sovereign powers that be, the Archduke had no choice but to swallow his indignation lest he commit himself to a conflict he could not win.

"That was hardly my implication, Herr Nero," the Archduke replied, his voice soft and free even of the pretence of warmth.

"Archduke, if I may?" I interjected. "If it is your sister's safety that concerns you, then why not hire professionals? Frankly, for what we charge, you could just as easily employ a Varangian, or even a *bushi*."

"That is not an option."

"Why not?"

"Because all mercenaries are loyal to coin, not contracts, Herr Valentine. They can be bought. That is why I am reaching out to you, now." The Archduke hit Nero with a scathing look. "While some may quibble about your methods, no one questions the principles of a Purifier."

"And what about your own guards?" I asked. "Surely you do not question their loyalty."

"Of course not. I have utter faith in my men. But allowing any of my household guard to accompany my sister to Constantinople would suggest I do not trust the Praetor to protect her."

"Which you clearly do not."

"Because I am not a fool. Herr Valentine, my family's bedrock is built on betrothal, not battle. My grandmother's marriage to the late Emperor averted an all-out war that would have swept up the entire world in its wake. This union may not have the same widespread repercussions, but it will bolster relations between Old Rome and New."

"And that is a bad thing because…"

"Because there are those determined to oppose that outcome. Some for overt political reasons, others for economic or even ideological ones. Worse, I know little of Constantinople's politics or its players. If I wish to ensure a warm welcome, I must visit and stoke the flames, myself. And that I cannot do with my sister in tow."

"Wait a moment, Your Grace," I said, raising a hand for emphasis. "You cannot mean to say this was your plan, all along? To hire us under false pretences so we might instead protect your sister?"

"No, Herr Valentine, I assure you the job is very real. There are…things happening at the dig site that no one can explain. But, in my country, we have a saying. *Was du allein wissen willst, das sage niemand.* Roughly translated, it means 'when you want something kept secret, tell no one.' For my plan to work, I could not risk tipping my hand. As I have already alluded to, the Praetor would no doubt take offence should my sister arrive surrounded by Habsburg guards or mercenaries. But he could hardly begrudge the presence of Purifiers, especially those performing their duty."

"Do you know what the life expectancy of a Purifier is, Your Grace?" I asked.

"I do not see what that has to do—"

"Humour me. Please."

"Very well. The answer is no, I do not."

"Two years. For some, it's a matter of months, maybe even weeks. Do you know why that is?"

"If you are suggesting your job is dangerous—"

"What I am suggesting is that your sister would be safer juggling grenadoes blindfolded than spending an hour in our disreputable company. Your Grace."

Nero eyed the nobleman. "Except that's not what His Grace has in mind, is it? You are planning to transfer the Archduchess to another skyship once we reach Cappadocia, then go on ahead to Constantinople to play politician."

"Which is where you and Herr Valentine will be expected to join me once your contract has been fulfilled, yes."

"And your sister," Nero added. "Who will just so happen to accompany us on that trip."

"Coincidentally, yes."

Nero grunted.

"It's a clever plan," I admitted. "Unless, of course, our routine investigation goes to shit, and the two of us end up dead."

The Archduke raised a forestalling hand. "Ah, but even were harm to befall the two of you, I would be duty bound to return to Cappadocia at first opportunity to discover for myself what went awry, at which point I could collect my sister, myself. Though it goes without saying that yours is the less likely scenario. After all, as Herr Valentine said, this is merely a routine investigation."

"I can see you've given this a great deal of thought, Archduke, and I can appreciate your plan's contingencies. But I cannot condone it. We do not want your coin."

"Herr Nero, please be reasonable—"

"However," Nero interrupted, scratching idly at the puckered skin of his throat, "if the Archduchess is headed to Constantinople on the same skyship we are, anyway, then I see no reason why we should not all travel together. She and Valentine are more or less acquainted now, are they not?"

Though I knew he meant it in jest, I could not help but experience a twinge of guilt at the thought. After having seen the Archduke's reaction to the mere suggestion of impropriety—not to mention the fact that the Archduchess was perhaps just north of fifteen and already being used as a political bargaining chip—I could appreciate both her melancholy and her desire to keep it to herself. After all, whatever anguish she endured, she endured for family.

"I believe that could be arranged, Herr Nero," the Archduke replied, thoughtfully. "And if something unexpected should occur during the journey?"

"Professionally speaking, I make no promises. Purifiers don't get involved in politics. But I'm not going to leave an innocent girl to be murdered because her brother was more worried about saving face than her safety, if that's what you're implying."

The Archduke pursed his lips. "I see. And you, Herr Valentine? Do you share his sentiments?"

"Which sentiment would that be? The one about your priorities, or the bit about rescuing damsels in distress?"

"The latter. Obviously."

Rather than reply immediately, I turned to admire the view from the observation deck I had heard so much about. Hundreds of feet below, the slate grey peaks of sprawling mountain ranges rose, their rippled summits ridged like slices of cheese carved by a dull knife while the sprawling ravines they formed crisscrossed the landscape like the thorny branches of a withered rose bush. Taken as a whole, the panorama was utterly breathtaking, albeit stark. And yet, I found myself dwelling on the staggering cost of such a view, especially considering how few were privileged enough to enjoy it.

"Herr Valentine?"

"My apologies, Your Grace. You wanted to know whether I will do as Nero has vowed and intercede should someone target the Archduchess?"

"In short, yes."

"I will not." I waved off the Archduke's reply. "Not without incentive, that is. You see, Your Grace, I am both far less scrupulous than my colleague and far less inclined to take risks for anyone's sake but my own. So, if it is all the same to you, let us talk coin."

V

INTERLUDE: THE FIVE FAMILIES

A few centuries or so past, the very air above our heads was sold and divided into chunks, later known as skylanes, in what most consider one of the riskiest financial gambits of all time. Entire nations were targeted in this enterprise, the majority of which were only too happy to accept the terms of the seemingly preposterous deal. In fact, so many welcomed the exchange that the buyers—a conglomerate of forward-looking manufacturers known forevermore as the Five Families of Florence—teetered on the edge of bankruptcy for almost a decade.

Over that span, the Five became a laughingstock throughout the Empire—the benchmark of every bad investment and the butt of many a joke. In the taverns, whenever a patron petitioned for a drink on the house, the barkeep would say, "What do you think this is, a Family establishment?" In the lending houses, debtors who managed to cover their expenses at the last minute called it "drawing sixth" in reference to those merchants who eschewed the mad venture.

Then the very first skyship launched.

And everything changed.

In the years that followed, the Five gained both tremendous wealth and considerable influence—so much so, in fact, that skylanes have become frontiers in their own right, their borders every bit as contested as those below. Indeed, most modern maps now come standard with overlays denoting which skylanes are held by which Family. Of late, it has even been suggested that these celestial territories may one day supersede their terrestrial counterparts, thereby forever shifting the balance of power.

Those who advocate for this possibility range anywhere from the enterprising machinist waiting in vain for the proceeds of his latest patent, to the industrial magnate who tires of propping up a thankless and incompetent government. The ideology they share is simple: for trade to thrive, trade must rule. To that end, there are some who have made it their life mission to accelerate this process by any means necessary.

These fundamentalists call themselves Mercantiles—or Mercs, for short.

VI

THE ENVY OF ANATOLIA

"We will be entering Cappadocia's skyport very shortly, Signori. Please return to your rooms and wait for a steward to inform you when we have docked. If either, or both, of you are staying on with us to Constantinople, we ask that you remain in your cabin until we ring the dinner bell so as to allow the other passengers time to disembark. If this is to be your last stop, we wish you a safe journey and sincerely hope you choose the Feretti family for all your transportation needs. *Valete*, Signori."

Nero and I leaned against the railing, ignoring the steward's long-winded diatribe so studiously he may very well have thought us deaf. He departed with a huff, leaving us to watch the skyship descend in peace from the otherwise deserted observation deck, each presumably lost in his own thoughts.

Mine were for the young Archduchess and her ill-fated marriage to perhaps the second most powerful man in the Empire—a reputedly ruthless tactician whose designs on Salamo's throne were the worst kept secret of our age. As for Nero, well, I dare not speculate. I never could tell what that man was thinking.

By the time I roused myself, I saw we were hemmed in on either side by sheer ridges, flying within spitting distance of those misshapen spires known as fairy chimneys. Signs of habitation began to emerge among the crags—evidence of the refuge this region had once provided for the tribes of persecuted Greeks who first settled this otherworldly place.

I watched the serpentine stairway which snaked from one cave entrance to the next—its smooth, windswept steps emerging so seamlessly from the rock it was as if nature had always intended for them to do so—speed past along with dozens of other such marvels. Having never recalled seeing any of it before, and certainly not from such heights, I found myself struck by the sheer obstinacy those refugees had shown—the resolve required to literally carve out a home for oneself.

Of course, it may as well have been the drawings of a primitive cave dweller compared to the vision that greeted us as the *Ex Machina* cleared the mountain pass and our intended destination came into view.

As grandiose as the mountain it was built on, the city of Cappadocia teemed with squat, blocky buildings hewn primarily from the stone itself. Most were dwellings piled atop each other like the seats of a crowded amphitheater—an urban sprawl which began at the foot of the mountain, swarmed up the slopes, and stopped yards from the summit, itself an ungainly hunk of honeycombed rock shaped like a hand with its fingers lopped off.

Beyond the city, the sun had only just begun its evening plunge, and yet the stunted windows and narrow doorways were already brimming with ventlight. Within the hour, ventlamps would blaze in every household, their viridescent flames steeping the entire city in variegated shades of green. This effect, coupled with Cappadocia's unique topography, had earned the unlikely metropolis a colourful nickname among those who cared more for aesthetics than accuracy—the Envy of Anatolia.

"You charged the Archduke out of spite."

Momentarily startled, I glanced at Nero before turning my attention back to the breathtaking view. "So what if I did?"

"It was foolish."

"Oh? So, what, I should have done the deed for free?"

"Men like the Archduke can spare the coin. In fact, he will sleep better knowing you took his money. The way he sees it, you owe him now."

"Perhaps you're right," I admitted, shrugging. "But I wanted to see what he was willing to pay. And now I know."

The old man grunted. "Next time, if there is a next time, ask for a favour instead. You may have survived the Culling, and you may even have what it takes to outlive me, but in all my years I have yet to come across anything more dangerous than a man with coin to waste and an axe to grind. Our office grants privileges, not immunity. Petra should have taught you that much, at least."

After firing that parting salvo, Nero straightened and withdrew. I watched him go from the corner of my eye, both stung by his remark and surprised at his salient advice. Not so long ago, I might have chosen to nurture the grievance, sulking until the sun rose. Now, however, I could at least admit he had a point; to truly make a man pay, one had to find the optimal currency.

It was simple arithmetic, really.

"Signore, I must ask that you join your companion below."

A glance over one shoulder revealed a middle-aged, heavyset steward with both hands clasped across his belly in the curious fashion of all those second-class citizens raised in the shadows of the Empire. Conspicuously absent, however, was the simpering posture and the veneer of congeniality one expected of an Auxiliary. If anything, the steward had the air of a soldier—retired, perhaps, or at the very least discharged.

"For your own safety," the steward added.

"Anticipating a rough landing?"

"Not particularly, Signore, though you cannot be certain in this part of the country. The *tempestas* are sometimes known to arrive without warning. Unfortunately, experience tells us even minor turbulence can result in major complications for our passengers. As they say: *causa latet, vis est notissima*. The cause may be hidden, but the result is well known. And we would hate to see a valued passenger hurt simply because we dismissed the possibility."

"Hurt, huh?" I glanced down at my hands for a moment where they gripped the rail, cataloguing the vast array of nicks and puckered scars that blanketed them—brief flashes of bar scraps and fistfights accompanied by memories of sand soaking up blood, of bones being reset and flesh sown, of staring eyes and lolling tongues.

"Signore, I do not wish to be rude, but I must insist," the steward continued, having apparently mistaken my silence for dissent. "If you do not return to your room at once, I will have no choice but to escort you there, myself. By force, if need be."

"Hmm?" I perked up at the thinly veiled threat, glanced down at the man's tightly clenched fists, and sighed. "That won't be necessary. I, too, would prefer not to see anyone hurt."

VII

THE ARCHAEOLOGIST

*A*t first glance, the dig site was little more than a gaping hole in the ground—a pit so deep not even the light of the noonday sun could pierce its gloomy depths. There was, however, evidence of prior industry: a rope ladder lying in a jumbled heap alongside an assortment of grimy, secondhand ventlamps, as well as an array of meticulously arranged wire brushes sitting atop a tarp secured at each corner by heavy stones, shielded from the wind by a bundle of what looked suspiciously like standard-issue firebrands bound in spikewire. Indeed, it seemed all that was missing from the site were the diggers themselves. Though, naturally, it was the presence of the contraband torches—not the absence of the labourers—that concerned Nero most.

"Those better not be what I think they are," he groused.

"I am sure the Archduke will have a good explanation," I replied, shrugging. "If not, we will get to see a nobleman arrested. That would be new."

The senior Purifier grunted and glanced over one shoulder, appraising the nobleman as he bid his sister—who had practically begged to accompany us on the first leg of our journey—farewell. An odd request, I felt, especially given how timid she had become since. Indeed, I caught the child peeking through the narrow gap in the curtain which separated the nobles and ourselves a handful of times, only to watch her eyes dart away like a pair of startled hummingbirds. But then, I suppose we must have been quite the novelty to a girl like her: two trained killers with neither land nor title whose authority was nonetheless recognised by emperors and kings alike.

The siblings embraced awkwardly, their affections appearing not so much strained as unfamiliar. The elder broke away first, patted his sister on the head like one might a small dog, and barked an order that sent the coachman scurrying to open the door. The Archduchess cast one last, lingering look at us before allowing herself to be herded into the whistlecoach's rear cabin.

"Herren Nero and Valentine," the Archduke called as he strode towards us, waving, "please forgive the delay. My man will no doubt have heard the whistlecoach and should be along any moment now."

"What I am willing to forgive, Archduke," Nero replied, "is very much up for debate at the moment. Tell me, what sort of operation are you running here, exactly?"

The Archduke squinted at us both as if trying to decide whether or not we were serious. "I am afraid you have me at a disadvantage, Herr Nero. To what do you refer?"

In reply, Nero pointed to the torches.

The Archduke tracked Nero's finger and visibly paled. He withdrew a handkerchief from the lining of his military jacket to dab at the perspiration peppering his brow, shaking his head so adamantly that the conspicuous medals pinned to his chest jounced and jangled.

"Well, Archduke?

"I assure you I have never seen those before in my life. I am not a fool. I would never defy Imperial law, and certainly not so brazenly as that."

"Then how do you explain them?"

"I cannot."

"Then who can?"

"I am not certain. The archaeologist in charge of the excavation, perhaps? Like you, this is my first time here."

"You mean to tell me you have never been to your own dig site?"

"I am the site's benefactor, Herr Nero. I pay the labourers to do what they are meant to do, and I pay those in charge to make sure the labourers know what that is. That is my role here. Were I to go beyond it, I would simply be in the way."

Nero sucked his teeth and passed me his satchel. He walked over and crouched down beside the bundle, presumably searching for a mark of manufacture. Not that it would tell us much; despite the consequences, low-grade knockoffs were known to make their way to the underground markets from lands outside Imperial control—poorer nations where fire oil and wood was cheaper to come by than refined infernite.

Nero gestured me over. "Valentine, come and tell me what this symbol says. My eyes aren't what they used to be."

"Do not touch those! They are mine!"

An absurdly spindly Germani strode towards us accompanied by a gaggle of native Cappadocians dressed in voluminous tunics that covered each from neck to toe in breathable cotton. A few wore headdresses in the Arabian style, leaving everything but their eyes covered, while others sported the brimless, tasseled caps made fashionable by the Greeks who settled here so long ago. All had dark features, though the cast of their skin ranged from beige to bronze.

"And who are you?" Nero asked, his grim tone undercut by the creaking of his joints as he rose.

"I might well ask you the same question!" The newcomer—another Germani, judging by his accent—fought to rid himself of the strands of white-blonde hair that clung to his damp forehead, clawing at them the way one might an errant spider's web. "How did you find this place, and what is it you want? I warn you, we can and will defend ourselves."

"Herr Doktor Adler!" the Archduke exclaimed, aghast.

"Your Grace?" The Germani bent forward, squinting until every crease in his middle-aged face became a veritable crevice. "Is that you?"

"Of course it is! Can you not see me standing here?"

As if on cue, a member of Adler's entourage tapped his shoulder and passed over a monocle with a lens so thick it might have been taken from the windowpanes of an observation deck. Adler grunted, slid the device into place, and blinked owlishly at the three of us for several seconds before folding at the waist in a bow so exaggerated that his monocle went rolling across the ground like a loose coin.

"*Gottverdammt!*" Adler scrambled to recover his renegade eyeglass, chasing after it so gracelessly that I thought he might never retrieve it.

Fortunately, the local who had passed over the monocle in the first place swooped in to help, deftly retrieving the lens and returning it to Adler. To my surprise, the eyes above the veil belonged to a woman—both slightly kohled and thickly lashed, they found mine and lingered even after she rejoined the others.

"Excuse me, Your Grace." Adler bowed a second time, though with greater care. "There have been reports of Armenians roaming the borders, not to mention those *verdammt* monks poking around. Perhaps had you sent word of your arrival, I would have known to expect you."

"I did. I sent you a post over a week ago, Herr Doktor, from the skyport in Alexandria."

"Did you?" Adler massaged the bridge of his nose. "I am sorry, Your Grace. The last few days have been especially...trying. There is much we need to discuss. Privately."

"That will not be necessary. So long as the excavation is what you wish to talk about, you may speak freely. These men are here to help."

"Oh?" Adler's superimposed eye swiveled back and forth between Nero and me. "I take that to mean you were successful, Your Grace?"

"It does. Herr Doktor Adler, allow me to introduce Herr Nero the Eighth and Herr Valentine the Ninth. Both come highly recommended."

"I should say so, Your Grace," Adler replied, jutting an overlong chin in Nero's general direction. "I never thought I would live to see a Purifier with gray hair. How remarkable you must be at your job to have survived so long!"

"I think you should be less concerned with me and more concerned with the explanation you owe us, Doktor. You claimed these firebrands were yours. Do you stand by that?"

"I do." Adler fluttered a hand at Nero as though they were discussing something far more trivial than treason. "There is no need to look so suspicious. I have a special dispensation from the Antiquities Guild, signed by Emperor Salamo himself. Twenty torches. Standard issue for a dig of this duration. I have logs, should you like to look over them. A man in my position can never be too careful."

"I would. But first, what position would that be?"

"Court Archaeologist. And no, before you ask, the job is far less glamorous than it sounds."

"Do not be so modest, Herr Doktor," the Archduke said. "Herr Doktor Adler is third in the line of succession to be named Imperial Historian. It is a highly coveted title that aristocrats and academics alike would die for. If you will pardon the expression."

"Impressive," Nero replied, though his tone suggested otherwise. "And what would a Court Archaeologist need torches for?"

"I believe that is my business."

"Herr Doktor, surely—" the Archduke began.

"Please, Your Grace. I do not answer to Herr Nero any more than he answers to me. I might as well inquire what a Purifier would need a fire-brand for."

"To kill that which refuses to die," Nero replied evenly, ticking down a finger at a time as he spoke. "Flames. Salt. Silver. Stone. Herbs. Those are our disciplines as well as our tools. Some work better than others, depending on the situation, but fire does the job more often than not."

Adler clapped his hands together. "So it does! Spoken like a true disciple. That must make you a *bestiarius*."

"It would," Nero admitted, gruffly.

"No need to look so surprised. I am a student of history, after all. I would have guessed as much given your title alone. Emperor Nero. The Great Fire. Very apt. And Valentine, was it? That is an odd one. Do you share his discipline?"

"No, Herr Doktor."

"I thought not. What does that make you, then? You are too slight to be a *scutarius*, surely. I doubt you could see past a shield that size. So not a disciple of Stone. Maybe a *dimachaerus*? A Silver?"

"Once," I replied, grudgingly. "But no longer. I'm a *scissor*."

"A Salt? Truly?" Adler looked taken aback. "I thought that discipline was banned centuries back."

"It was. It's a rather long story."

"And one I should very much like to hear, I think."

The Archduke cleared his throat, loudly. "Is someone going to tell me what in Caesar's name you are talking about?"

"Nothing that should concern you, Archduke," Nero replied. "Nor any of us, at present."

"Herr Nero is correct, Your Grace," Adler added. "I got carried away, as we academics so often do. Forgive me."

"I do sympathise, Herr Doktor. But, in case it has escaped your notice, it is very hot and already past midday. Perhaps we should move on to more pressing matters."

"Of course!" Adler slapped his forehead. "What a fool I am, Your Grace. I should have suggested we retire from the first, forgive me. Come, the valley is not far. We can speak of what has happened as we walk."

Nero inserted himself between the two Germani with a forestalled hand. "You still have not answered my question, Doktor."

"Too right, Herr Nero. You wish to know why I have so many torches in my possession? The answer is that they are a precaution. A contingency should our diggers come across a deposit of infernite. A raw deposit, that is."

Nero and I exchanged startled glances. Encountering a fresh vein of crude infernite was a notoriously calamitous event. One part natural disaster and one part momentous discovery, such finds initially led to mass hysteria, mass displacement, and—more often than not—all-out war. It had been forty odd years since the last deposit was found, and already there were talks of which nation would seize control of the next one.

"That is not what happened here," Adler assured us. "Merely a possibility we must contend with."

"And what are the odds that it does?" Nero asked.

"Long," Adler admitted. "It has happened only twice that I am aware of, and both were quite small finds. Still, one can never be too careful."

"And the torches?"

"We use them to monitor the quality of the air. If the flame expands or, Caesar forbid, turns green, then we know the site is contaminated. We task someone to watch it at all times and cry out should either event occur, which gives those below time to evacuate."

"Not bloody likely," I muttered, shaking off memories Adler's comments had conjured up: visions of men pouring from a steaming hole in the ground, their eyes and ears caked with slimy green tar, their flesh swarming with weeping lesions. Those who had survived long enough to scream were later found drowned, their lungs filled with blood the colour of the Thames. A minor leak, that was what the Bloodbacks had called it. Nothing to see here, boy, move along—their words, spoken without sympathy or remorse.

"Did you say something, Herr Valentine?"

"No one would survive," I replied, doing my utmost to avoid eye contact. "If you tapped a vein, even a minor one, everyone in that hole would die. Fast, if they were lucky. Slow, if they weren't."

"Seen what the awful stuff can do for yourself, have you?" Adler asked.

"I grew up in Londinium."

"Ah, the Vents. That makes sense. You have my condolences. The city had its charms, once. Before they started mining and the Gallic States got involved."

"So I heard," I replied, reminded of Signore Garza for the first time in many years.

"Have you been back since the Emperor signed the trade agreement with the Iron Colonies? Rumour has it things have been much improved since, now that so many goods flow through Britannia."

"I have not, no."

"Perhaps this can wait, Herr Doktor?" The Archduke wrung out an already sweat-soaked handkerchief, his exasperation plain.

"Yes, of course. Shall we walk, Herr Nero?"

The senior Purifier agreed, and within moments the four of us were moving away from the excavation site, trailed by the archaeologist's entourage. I lagged a pace or two behind, content to listen and observe. Indeed, it was a duty I embraced; no matter how many decades have passed since my childhood, I remain most myself when no one is paying attention to me or my idle hands. Or, as Nero liked to say: *Semper iterum fur ferum.*

Once a thief, always a thief.

Adler cleared his throat. "It may save us some time to know how much the Purifiers already know, Your Grace."

"I passed along everything you mentioned in your letters. The unexplained phenomena and so on. I thought it best not to spare any details, given what is at stake for both of us should this venture go...poorly."

"Indeed." Adler pursed his lips thoughtfully. "Then you know what we were dealing with last week. Unfortunately, it seems those episodes were but the beginning. We have come across something much worse since His Grace and I were last in contact."

For a moment, Adler fell silent.

"A terrible sickness of some kind has taken most of the men," he continued. "None of whom I expect will survive more than a few days, and that is assuming their condition does not worsen."

The Archduke froze in his steps, halting us all with outstretched arms. "Why was I not told of this immediately?"

The woman who had come to his rescue earlier reached out to surreptitiously squeeze the archaeologist's shoulder—a reassuring gesture that spoke of a deeper relationship between the two. Adler removed his monocle and proceeded to clean it on his sleeve before replying.

"Until recently, I was unsure whether we were all afflicted, or soon to be. I could not risk sending a runner, nor could I afford to prematurely alert the citizens of Cappadocia. We depend on their supplies. If they were to shun us, we would face an even greater crisis. It was never my intention to mislead you, Your Grace, but the well-being of my people came first."

"Are you contagious?" the Archduke asked, stepping clear of the rest of us as though we were already plagued.

"I do not believe so, Your Grace. Thus far, the symptoms have been confined to those who fell ill that day. Though I would be a fool if I did not warn you to keep your distance and avoid unnecessary contact once we reach the valley."

"Have you no idea what you're dealing with?" Nero asked.

"I do not. It is an unnatural illness unlike any I have ever seen. Though, to be honest, I am so far out of my depth that I cannot begin to speculate. My talents lie in the study of ruins, not ruined men. I can only pray your arrival brings with it more answers than I have been able to find on my own. Of course, now that you know what awaits us, I will understand if any of you wish to turn back."

We each stood silent, compelled to weigh the value of their own lives against those of strangers. For me, it was not a difficult decision; I had seen plenty of death in my time, not to mention a great deal of sickness, and was frightened by neither.

"In that case," I said blithely, feigning a cheerfulness I did not feel, "I believe the saying goes *Des Teufels liebstes Möbelstück ist die lange Bank*, does it not?"

Both the Archduke and the archaeologist gaped at me, struck perhaps by my flawless pronunciation of the Germani proverb—a censure against procrastination which, when literally translated, goes "the Devil's favourite piece of furniture is the long bench." Nero, of course, was too busy shaking his head to appear surprised. But then he alone could appreciate the irony, given my proclivity for dithering. That, and he happened to have served alongside the miserable bastard who had drilled that particular phrase into the head of every would-be Purifier over the last two decades—the highest-ranking member and current head of our Order, Octavian V.

"You are not concerned for your own health, Herr Valentine?" The Archduke asked.

I shrugged. "People get sick. We all die. What separates the wheat from the chaff is how much they whine about it."

"Valentine's right," Nero said. "There's no sense delaying further. Lead on, Herr Doktor. If your men can bear their suffering, then we can bear to witness it."

VIII

THE VALLEY & THE VARANGIAN

*T*he smell hit us first.

It was a metallic odor, copper-tinged and intermingled with a malodorous foetor that made it difficult to swallow without wanting to cough or spit. If the archaeologist and his entourage noticed it, they made no comment. Neither did Nero, though I knew for a fact his olfactory senses were at least as good as my own. The Archduke, meanwhile, held his damp handkerchief clamped so tightly over his nose and mouth that I doubted he could smell anything beyond his own sweat. Still, if he did, he said nothing.

Apparently, no one wished to acknowledge the stench, or, more accurately, to acknowledge we were headed towards its source.

After a few minutes, our progress was accompanied by the raucous song of monstrous crickets the size of my bloody palm—an indigenous species known colloquially as spiked magicians thanks to the mesmerizing way they moved their barbed forelimbs to lure unsuspecting prey. I remember thinking it too early for them to be about; overhead, the afternoon sun was a blazing force beating upon our backs, its oppressive heat offset only by the knowledge that our destination was just beyond the ridge we were ascending.

We halted at the top, mopping our brows with our sleeves and catching our collective breaths. Below, nestled on all sides by overlapping ridges,

Adler's valley lay before us—a partially shaded clearing largely sheltered from the gusting winds of the *tempestas*. A cluster of open-faced tents with camel skin roofs and patterned blankets for walls dotted the landscape, though my eyes were drawn to the patchwork monstrosity some hundred feet to the west—four times as large any of the others, the sprawling tent could have fit all of us and a dozen families, besides.

"How'd you get that all the way out here?" Nero asked, eyeing the tent.

"Not cheaply," Adler admitted. "But the investment is quite worth it. She is large enough to house any artifacts we find, many of which are too valuable to leave out in the open, and provides shelter from the storms."

"She does, does she?"

"Did, Herr Nero," Adler corrected as we reached the clearing, ignoring the Purifier's sarcasm. "Now, she looks over dying men. Come, we can rest once we have reached the bottom."

As we descended, those lusty chirps died away, supplanted by moans and whimpers carried on the foul air—an inharmonious blend of muffled pleas and pitiful groans that typified the symphony we call suffering. I had heard it before, more times than I could count. Some, of course, were more memorable than others, like that time we dropped anchor outside a plague-riddled Syracuse and watched it burn, or that time I found the room in the Sanitorium where they kept the pretty ones after they broke. Such were the orchestras and opera houses of my childhood.

And the Order wonders why I kill so easily.

"Ah, we have been spotted," Adler said, gesturing to one side of the valley where a colossal figure was only just emerging from one of the less formidable tents—a man so tall he had to duck to avoid hitting his head on the canopy.

"Caesar preserve us," the Archduke hissed. "That is a Varangian!"

"A retired Varangian, Your Grace. There is nothing to fear. Rurik works for us. I asked that he stay behind to defend the sick in our absence."

"Retired or not," I said, "a Varangian has many reasons to be feared."

Adler eyed me strangely before snapping his fingers. "Of course, you are a Britannian. *Scheisse.* Forgive me, I should have mentioned I had a Varangian in my employ."

"What is this, now? More Purifier nonsense?" The Archduke's expression was hidden behind the paisley pattern of his silken hanky, though the look in his eyes was clearly not that of a happy man.

"Not at all, Your Grace. There is a long-standing...grudge between Herr Valentine's people and Rurik's that goes back several decades."

"You're mistaken, Herr Doktor," I interjected, amused. "There's no grudge. To be honest, the Varangians are all but revered on our isle. We speak of them rarely, and in hushed voices like one would of vengeful gods, afraid they'll smite us for running our mouths."

"Smite you?" The Archduke looked down his nose at me—a haughty stare only partially undermined by the copious beads of sweat dribbling into his eyes. "Surely you are mistaken, Herr Valentine. That is reserved for God, and God, alone. As is our reverence."

"I have no interest in debating theology with you, Archduke. But just look at him. Look, and picture a beach teeming with such men, each of them outfitted and well-armed. Try to see them not as a noble might, but as a common man too weak to have been sent to war. A lame fisherman, perhaps, or a sickly tailor. Imagine how it must have felt to stand against such beasts armed with only nets and sewing needles, certain beyond all doubt that your odds of survival are no better than those of an insect in the shadow of a falling boot. And then tell me, Your Grace, what are gods if not beings vastly superior to any you have ever seen?"

Everyone fell silent, their attention shifting from me to the Varangian over the course of my little monologue. My point became increasingly salient the closer Rurik got, for the Varangian towered over all of us except Nero, who himself was descended from the Visigoths who conquered Hispania. Of course, the effect was somewhat tempered by the giant's awkward gait—a limp which at least partially explained what he was doing here and not on the frontlines fighting to secure the Empire's interests abroad.

When at last he arrived, I saw that the Varangian had the pale eyes and chestnut mane shared by a fair number of the children born in the first year after the rebellion had been put down—each one left behind to remind the survivors what being conquered truly meant. Indeed, I found myself wondering whether this man had been amongst those who raped and pillaged their way up and down Britannia.

"Rurik," Adler began, "these are our guests. This is our benefactor, Archduke Joseph Benedictus of the Habsburg Family. And these are his companions, Herr Nero the Eighth and Herr Valentine the Ninth."

"Purifiers."

That one word hung in the air like an accusation. The Varangian glow-ered at us as he pawed at his bushy beard and tugged on the ends of his moustache.

"Is that a problem?" Nero asked.

In answer, the Varangian lunged forward onto his good leg, swinging at the senior Purifier with a single, meaty fist. To my surprise, Nero managed to duck the haymaker, narrowly avoiding what might otherwise have been a jaw-breaking strike.

"Rurik!" Adler shouted, sounding absolutely mortified. "What do you think you are doing?!"

As if on cue, the Varangian lurched upright and raised both hands like a guilty child, his lopsided smile revealing a mouth riddled with missing teeth. For a moment, I assumed the big bastard was unhinged—one of those crazed soldiers who see war no matter where they look. But then I realised Nero, too, was grinning.

"It has been a long time, Nero," Rurik said, his thick, Thracian accent utterly at odds with his fair complexion. "I heard you were dead."

"Funny," Nero replied. "I heard the same about you. So, you were finally discharged."

"I prefer to think of it as forcibly retired."

Nero grunted a laugh. "Not much use for a veteran who cannot fight and refuses to lead, is that it?"

"Something like that."

"Was it the leg?"

"No, that came later. It was the hand. My fingers." Rurik held up three mangled digits on his right hand, the joints swollen and twisted. "I kept dropping my axe once the fighting started. I tried switching to my left, but I was sloppy. Bad footwork. Blew out my knee."

"Shame."

"Yes, well, you know what they say." Rurik held both arms wide, his wingspan nearly double my own, and shrugged. "*Quod scripsi, scripsi.* What's written is written. Besides, I like my new job. Or I did, until this madness started."

Adler took this as his cue. "And would one of you care to tell me how you two know each other? Herr Nero? Rurik?"

The two men exchanged amused glances.

"You tell them," Nero insisted. "You always enjoyed running your mouth."

Rurik barked a laugh and did what he was asked. From him, we learned their unlikely friendship had been forged some years back while the Varangian was posted in Caledonia, at which point a literal witch-hunt had led Nero to the doorstep of the local garrison. The tale that followed—a story of one man's relentless pursuit of a creature that was neither entirely human nor entirely monstrous—was one I had never before heard. Nero was characteristically tight-lipped throughout, speaking only to correct some gross exaggeration on Rurik's part.

"You should have seen him track that witch," Rurik continued. "He chased her north of the Wall and back again. A shame so little was left of her once he was done. She was one of the most beautiful women I have ever laid eyes on, and I have seen every whore from here to Londinium."

"Have you, now?" I asked, my interest piqued.

Nero held up his hand. "That is enough storytelling for one day. If we dally much longer, we will lose the light. Valentine, why don't you go and see what ails the men in that tent while Rurik and the Doktor fill me in on the details of what happened here?"

"You sure you don't want to see them for yourself?"

"I trust you know what to look for."

"Fair enough," I replied placidly.

"And what am I to do, Herr Nero?" the Archduke asked, cocking an eyebrow. "Or did you simply forget to order me about as you have everyone else?"

"On the contrary, I assumed you would do whatever you pleased, Archduke. I would never presume to tell a nobleman how to fill his precious time."

"Actually, Your Grace," Adler said, his tone soothing, "I was hoping you might join Herr Valentine. It would greatly reassure the men to know someone like you has come to help. Plus, you may have some invaluable insights we have not yet considered."

"I do not know about that, Herr Doktor, but if it will ease their suffering, I will gladly do so. Let me be clear about one thing, however. Nothing of our business arrangement should be discussed in front of Herr Nero or your Varangian. Is that understood? That is between us, and us, alone."

"Of course, Your Grace." The archaeologist bowed and waved at the woman in his entourage with one hand while gesturing between the nobleman and myself with the other. "Take these two on through, my dear, and answer any questions they may have."

The woman bowed her head.

Nero tapped me on the shoulder as we turned to go. "Once you've seen all you need to see, hurry back. I have a bad feeling this job has just gotten a lot more complicated since we took it."

"So serious," Rurik remarked, studying his old friend. "The last time I saw your face that grim, you were about to set fire to a house full of acolytes."

"Let's hope it does not come to that."

The uncomfortable silence that accompanied Nero's reply stretched on for so long that I decided to walk away rather than endure it. Of course, I did not need to remain behind to picture the fear reflected in the eyes and faces of Adler's people, nor to imagine what it must be like for them with their mundane horrors and everyday tragedies to hear that their friends and loved ones could so easily be reduced to ashes and dust.

I was a child once, after all.

IX

THE CURSE

I held open the tent flap and slipped inside, struck at once by the strength of the odor at its source—a coppery stench so overwhelming I had to shield my nose and mouth with my sleeve to keep from gagging. Overhead, sunlight spread across the canopy without ever actually piercing the canvas, leaving the interior both dim and surprisingly cool. I heard a rustling from behind as the Archduke and Adler's guide followed me into the tent, their shadows stretching the length of the dirt floor before the flap fell shut behind them.

"I can hardly see anything in here," the Archduke complained. "Someone turn on a light."

The guide moved away, the sound of her shuffling footsteps quickly supplanted by the peal of metal on metal and the telltale grind of a ventlamp's crank. Seconds later, a shaft of emerald light pierced the gloom, and I found myself surrounded by dying men.

They lay on camp beds, sprawled on their backs or curled up on their sides beneath sheets that might have been white once but were now soiled brown with dried blood and sweat. Or so I had assumed; when our guide hung the ventlamp on a nearby rafter, I realised that what I had mistaken for bodily fluids were in fact corrosive stains—greasy splotches that shimmered faintly whenever the patients tossed or turned.

The pale lips of the patient nearest me, a young man with dark, matted curls splayed across his forehead, twitched when I bent over to examine him. When my shadow fell across his face, he whimpered like a beaten dog, rolling away from me and tugging free the sheet pinned across his upper body to reveal a shoulder caked in what looked like metallic paint that had begun to fleck. I peered closer, unsure what I was seeing.

The young man shifted, and a metal shard roughly the size of a toenail fell away from that shoulder, landing on the floor with an audible clink. Startled, I stared at the divot it left behind—an indentation deep enough that blood should already have welled to the surface—only to notice dozens more just like it, his flesh pockmarked in so many places it was as though a sculptor had been chipping away at him to find a more pleasing form.

I straightened and shook my head. I had seen such afflictions before, of course. I had spent a great deal of my life in cities where such diseases were commonplace, though admittedly this seemed a far cry stranger than the weeping sores or scaly hives I had encountered in the past.

A couple beds away, the Archduke made a choked noise and backed away from an elderly digger who had reached out with a gnarled metal knob where his hand should have been. The digger stayed like that for a few seconds, straining with every muscle in his aging body before promptly passing out. His leaden fist struck the ground with a sickening thud.

"This was a mistake." The Archduke waved his handkerchief in surrender. "Whatever their affliction, I dare not risk joining these men. It was foolish of me to accompany you, Herr Valentine. Please, return when you are finished with your inspection. I will join the others outside."

The Archduke brushed past our guide with a mumbled apology and staggered through the opening with one hand pressed to his gut as though he might vomit. Our guide moved to close the flap he had thrown wide in his desperation, moving with a calm assurance that cast an unflattering light on the Archduke's abrupt departure—like watching a grown man cower before a portentous shadow while a mere child looked on with resolve.

"Can you tell me what exactly happened to these men?" I asked, my voice hushed so as not to disturb those around me.

"We were hoping you might tell us."

To my surprise, the woman's accent was quite similar to Adler's, albeit a tad farther south in dialect. There was also an inexplicable bite to her words —a surliness bordering on contempt that I neither understood nor appreciated. Sadly, hers was hardly an uncommon reaction; at this point in my life, I considered open hostility an occupational hazard.

"I have never seen anything like it," I admitted, opting for a more conciliatory tone. "But that was not what I meant. I don't expect you to know what this is. If you did, Adler would have told us already. What I want to know is when this all began. What were the first symptoms? Who got sick first? Adler said you would provide—"

"My father," the guide interrupted, "sent you in here as a courtesy, nothing more. He asked the Archduke to find experts who could help us determine what was happening at our excavation site, not to hire thugs. This disease is not something your kind can help us with. What our people need most right now are doctors, not killers."

"Is that so?"

"Am I wrong? You already admitted you do not know what this sickness is, which means—"

"On the contrary, Fraulein, that is not what I said. I said I had never seen anything like it. But that does not mean I am incapable of speculating."

"Then speculate."

I started to reply, then hesitated. If my hunch was right, it would mean a great deal of trouble for everyone involved, especially if word of this mysterious affliction reached the ears of my superiors. Still, I would only be delaying the inevitable; if I did not voice these suspicions, someone would. It was only a matter of time.

"I believe it is a curse," I said. "In fact, I am very nearly certain of it."

"A curse? You must be joking. There are no such things as curses."

"They are rare, I will grant you that. Very rare. The art has been lost, but I assure you the oldest and most powerful of them still exist. They cling to specific objects or manifest in certain bloodlines. Occasionally, they have been known to ruin entire harvests or to wipe out entire villages..." I drifted off, eyeing the dozens of occupied beds.

Adler's daughter tracked my gaze. "If you are right, and I am not admitting you are, would that explain why the care we have given them seems to have done nothing?"

"If I'm right," I allowed, "then yes, it means traditional medicine will do next to nothing. Ailments like these are usually a matter for priests, not physicians."

"And what about their symptoms?"

"What about them?"

"How do you explain them? Just look at their skin! It has become hard as stone and brittle as cast iron. What manner of curse does that?"

"I am afraid I do not know. How fast has this rash of theirs been spreading?"

"Rash?"

"I could not think of a better word."

Adler's daughter sighed and shook her head. "It spread quickly, at first. But it slowed considerably ever since we returned them to camp. Would a curse do that?"

"It could. Most curses are strongest near their source. Which, judging by the fact that your father has all but abandoned it, would be the dig site. Is it something you uncovered, perhaps?"

"That I do not know. All I can tell you is that the excavation site is where they all were when this happened. But wait!" She took a step closer, her voice suddenly hopeful. "Does that mean that if we were to move them farther away from here, they would recover?"

"Regrettably, no. At least there is no evidence to support that conclusion. According to the literature, curses must be lifted. They cannot be cured, nor run from. A slower, more agonizing death is still death."

"Did you say the literature? You mean you have no practical experience with this sort of thing?"

"I did mention curses are rare, did I not?" I held up my hand to forestall her reply. "Listen, you were right to call us killers, before. But that's not all we are, nor is it all we are trained to do. If you want to help these men, I need you to tell me what you know. Please."

Adler's daughter turned away as though to study the faces gathered at our feet, her shoulders slumped. When at last she replied, however, it was with the cool detachment of a surgeon speaking to a patient, or that of a weary barrister quoting precedent.

"They all fell ill at the same time. Or near enough, anyway, that it would be impossible to know otherwise. We had only recently uncovered a large chamber in the third quadrant, near the southwest marker, and these were the men working to secure the entrance. When—"

"*Chrysós...*"

The unfamiliar word emerged like a death rattle from the mouth of the young man I had inspected earlier, startling me so much I jumped. When I glanced down, however, I saw he remained fast asleep, his breathing shallow but otherwise regular. I cocked an eyebrow.

"What was that he said?"

"*Chrysós.* It is Greek. For gold." The woman shook herself. "He must be dreaming. Anyway, when the men came back up at the end of their shift, they were as you see them. Weak, unsteady. Delirious, in many cases."

"And their skin?"

"We did not notice the rash, as you called it, not at first. Everyone assumed it was bad air, or perhaps fatigue from the heat. It can be draining work down there, especially when you are breaking new ground. It was not until my father and the other men saw what lay beneath their thawbs that they began to suspect it was something more."

"And you are sure no one who has come into direct contact with them has fallen ill? Not even those who touched the diseased flesh?"

"None, though my father has insisted we keep our distance except to bring water and food."

"And what does your father think happened to these men?"

"He would not say," she admitted. "He will be interested to hear your talk of curses, though."

"He will?"

"My father has always been a superstitious man. His fondness for myths and legends is what led him to become an archaeologist. Deep down, I believe he is a romantic who thinks every ruin haunted until proven otherwise."

I scoffed at that. "Clearly your father has never experienced a genuine haunting, or he would not be so eager."

"I would not be so sure. Some would say that what we experienced here more than qualifies."

"What about you?"

"Me?"

"Yes. Are you one of those people?"

She took a deep breath and let it out slow. "I am no fool. I know ghosts exist. In fact, thanks to my father and his obsession with them, I know far more about their behaviours than most. And I will admit there were...incidents. A sense of lost time, missing equipment, even the occasional unexplained disappearance. But everyone and everything was eventually found, and no one was harmed."

"Until they were."

"Until they were," she allowed.

"So, what was different about that day? You said they were breaking new ground? Did they stumble across something while they were down there? A relic, perhaps, or something written on the walls?"

"That I do not know," she replied, her tone tinged with bitterness. "The men are far too addled to speak of what they saw, and my father forbade the rest of us from going down and investigating ourselves until we learned more about what happened and why."

"Smart," I acknowledged. "Very smart."

"Why do you say it like that?"

"Because, in my experience, people rarely do the smart, cautious thing. They usually do the dumb, reckless thing. Occasionally the clever, reckless thing. Either way, it does not often end well. Whatever his reasons, your father may have kept this curse from claiming a lot more lives."

"What about the men here who are already sick? Will we be able to save them?"

I turned to study the man at my feet, staring down at his discoloured flesh with the knowledge that—were the curse to spread any further—not even an amputation would save him. Assuming the rest were similarly afflicted, that left us with only two options: we could either find a way to lift this mysterious curse, or we could fill that bloody hole in the ground with dirt and burn this tent down with every last one of these poor souls still inside. Unfortunately, my vote did not count, and I could not be entirely sure which way Nero would lean.

"We should get back," I said, diplomatically.

X

LIES

Outside, a palpable tension rode the air. Off to our right, beneath the sloped canopy of a pagoda, Adler and the Archduke were engaged in a muted dispute of some sort. To our left, Nero and Rurik surveyed the landscape with their backs turned while Adler's people huddled in a tight cluster not a couple dozen feet away, their gazes oscillating nervously between both duos.

"What happened here?" I wondered aloud.

"Something is wrong. I should speak with my father. Excuse me, Herr Valentine."

"Wait, please." I halted Adler's daughter with an outstretched arm. "I wanted to thank you for taking the time to speak with me, Fraulein Adler. I'm sorry I could not be of more immediate assistance, but I swear I will do whatever I can to help."

Adler's daughter searched my face, her gaze nearly level with my own. We stood like that for perhaps a minute—me with an arm extended and her trying to decide if I was being sincere—and then, like two dancers performing the final movements of a familiar routine, we separated. I let my arm drop, and she looked away.

"Kissa," she said, her expression hidden away beneath the veil of her headdress. "Call me Kissa, please."

"I...of course."

Kissa gathered up the folds of her cloak as though to leave, only to wheel upon me with a furrowed brow. "You are not what I hoped you would be, Herr Valentine."

"Just Valentine is fine," I replied. "And, again, I'm sorry to disappoint."

"You did nothing of the sort."

I stared after the woman as she left to join her father, struck by the oddest sensation that I had missed something over the course of our exchange. There had been no flirtation, no teasing. No overtures of any kind, in fact. Nothing like what I had come to expect from the alehouse strumpets with their salacious suggestions, or the bright-eyed petticoats with their coquettish looks and constant fidgeting.

And yet.

"What was that about?" Nero asked, his silent approach startling me from my private thoughts.

"Honestly? I am not entirely sure."

"Anything I should be concerned about?"

"No, nothing like that."

"Good. You would not want to upset an Anatolian, Valentine. They hold grudges the way executioners hold axes."

"I had not planned on it. Besides, that woman isn't local. She's Adler's daughter."

"Ah. So, she's the one."

I turned and arched an eyebrow.

"It's nothing," Nero said, waving my look away. "Something Rurik mentioned in passing, that's all. It does not matter. So, was it as bad in there as it smells?"

"Worse," I admitted.

I quickly summarised my conversation with Kissa, though I kept my own observations to a minimum as Nero had always preferred to come to his own conclusions. Of course, I could tell by the questions he asked and the grim look on his face that he agreed with me. Once I was finished, he drew me aside and insisted we take a walk.

"I need you to do something for me, Valentine," Nero began after a moment's silence, his gravelly, humorless voice so hushed I had to pick up the pace just to hear him. "You won't like it."

"You would make a terrible solicitor, Nero. Has anyone ever told you that?"

"Constantinople," he said, ignoring my jibe. "I need you to go there. I've arranged for you to leave with the Archduke first thing in the morning. He's agreed to secure passage for you both on the first departing flight. I made sure to tell him you weren't picky about where you sleep."

"Of course you did," I deadpanned, reminded yet again of Nero's enterprising cruel streak. "And why do you want me to go to New Rome?"

"Before we get into that, there are a few things you need to know." Nero squinted up at the sky, the crinkled flesh around his eyes spreading like fissures down his cheeks. "The Archduke did not hire Doktor Adler to oversee some excavation out in the middle of nowhere. He was hired to dig up information on the Cappadocian priests and their terra-cotta recipe. The man is a spy."

I had to study Nero's face to see if he was joking; the senior Purifier had a bizarre sense of humour that often left me feeling flat-footed and vaguely disturbed. I could see immediately, however, that he was not. Still, I found his assertion hard to believe.

"A spy?" I frowned, picturing the spindly, bumbling academic. "Are you sure? The man seems far too...indelicate for that sort of thing."

"I believe that's the point. You should know by now that we have a tendency to overlook those we think beneath us. It's what you counted on as a child picking people's pockets. Clearly, the Doktor knows that, too. He plays the role of the buffoon much the same way you do that of the layabout."

"That isn't—"

"It is a clever choice on his part," Nero went on, cutting off my protestations. "Archaeologists can go almost anywhere in the world without being questioned or molested, especially when supported by a reputable patron. Planning an excavation gives Adler an excuse to speak with the locals, reach out to tribal leaders, and even map the area without raising suspicion. Combine all that with some feigned incompetence, and, even were he to be caught sticking his nose where he shouldn't, he could easily blame it on a misunderstanding or a cultural misstep."

"You sound impressed."

"I am." Nero adjusted his pack, slinging it round so it bounced off his left thigh and not his right. "Do you know, Valentine, what separates the good spies from the great ones?"

"The great ones don't get caught?"

"Close," Nero replied. "A good spy can don the mask at a moment's notice. They can become anything they need to be to suit the situation. But a great spy? A great spy never takes the mask off."

"I am not sure I follow," I confessed.

"A good spy can be *anything*, but not necessarily *anyone*. They may dress and behave like a noble, but that doesn't mean they could impersonate one. There are too many things you cannot fake. Credentials, relationships, accomplishments. And Adler has them all."

"Ah. You're implying Adler uses his position and his connections to obtain information while simultaneously building a reputation as a renowned archaeologist."

Nero nodded approvingly. "I doubt even his crews know how he secures his funding, or what his real agendas are."

"Do you think his daughter knows?"

"It would be difficult to keep a secret like that from family, but not impossible. Why, did she say something?"

"Not about her father, but I got the sense she takes issue with our being here. Or perhaps with us. It would hardly be the first time."

"Nor the last, I wager."

"What did Adler have to say about the dig site?" I asked, hoping to change the subject. "I assume he knew better than to break cursed ground."

"The archaeologist insists he heard a rumour about this place from a man in Athens."

"You don't believe him?"

Nero shrugged. "I think it more likely he chose this place for its convenience. We are close enough to Cappadocia that his people could travel back and forth without raising suspicion while also being remote enough to discourage visitors."

"If that's true, then the Doktor has some truly awful luck."

"I could be wrong. Maybe he did hear a rumour. Or perhaps he suspected something was here all along and used the Archduke's coin to fund his dig. All I know is that they stumbled upon something down there. Something valuable. And that is when the haunting started."

"So it was a haunting."

"Or something to do with the curse. We won't know for certain until we locate the source."

"Could it be this treasure they found?"

"I doubt it. The timeline doesn't match up. Besides, if what they found was cursed, I assume Adler himself would have fallen ill by now. He's got it hidden away somewhere under lock and key."

"What is it?"

"Never got a chance to ask. Once the Archduke overheard there was something of real value down there, he pulled Adler away. They've been arguing ever since. I expect the Archduke will try to claim whatever it is for himself. He'll be wanting anything that might offset his losses."

"Typical."

Nero nodded. "He may be an arrogant, greedy bastard, but he has a sharp mind for business. And he clearly isn't afraid to get his hands dirty, or he never would have hired Adler in the first place. If there is a way to profit from this mess, he is likely to find it."

"I assume he's hoping we will lift the curse so he can take credit for the find?"

"And for saving the diggers. If we were to succeed, he'd be hailed as the hero who hired us to cure them. When you think about it, that is the only way he comes out of this with his reputation intact."

"And can we? Save them, I mean." I caught the slightest twitch of Nero's moustache as a deep scowl formed beneath his whiskers. "You're worried the Order will insist we abandon them, aren't you? Or have they done so already? Is that why they sent us? Because they knew we would do their dirty work?"

"Of course not."

"I knew there was something off about this job!" I hissed, shaking my head. "Damn you, Nero, I gave my word we would at least try to help these people. Were you even going to tell me, or were you just going to start setting fires and digging graves?"

"You're letting that wild imagination of yours get the better of you, boy. I told you, that is not what's going on here."

"Then what is it? And I want the whole truth this time. Unless you don't trust me. Is that it?"

Rather than reply, Nero picked up his pace, his impossibly long stride making it difficult to keep up without jogging after him—something I was loath to do. Instead, I trailed after him, focusing on the rugged scenery while I struggled to rein in my sudden suspicions.

The valley had a stark beauty to it, the sort that could be easily overlooked in the midday heat but became more and more obvious as the sun waned and the pale blue sky beyond the ridges bled orange and bruised purple. Of course, that meant the darkness of the wilderness—a smothering blanket of night that stretched on for miles, beneath which all manner of creatures prowled—was also on its way.

And that I was less than thrilled about.

Up ahead, Nero slowed. He retrieved a wad of waxy paper filled with resin from the breast pocket of his waistcoat, unwrapped it, and plopped a sticky blob of it into his mouth. When I caught up to him, he offered me some. I declined, and for a while the terse silence continued, interrupted only by the crunch of our steps and the rhythmic clenching of Nero's jaw.

"I do trust you," Nero said, at last. "I trust you in a fight, and to do your job. If I didn't, I would have let you get yourself killed a long time ago."

"Then why—"

"Hush." Nero spat to one side. "You wanted the truth, so I am giving it to you. First, the Order did not send us out here. I volunteered."

"You did? But why?"

"I owed an old friend a favour."

"Rurik," I said, realization dawning.

Nero nodded. "He wrote to me before the Archduke came knocking on our door. Rurik has been working for the archaeologist for a few years now and convinced the man to send for experts. For us. That's how I know what Adler really is and why he's really here."

"Why not tell me all this from the beginning?"

"It was need-to-know. This was supposed to be a haunt. All we needed to do was show up, investigate, and consecrate some ground. The last thing I wanted was to get involved in a nobleman's schemes."

"Did you know the Archduke planned to accompany us?"

"I suspected he might. He has a lot to lose here, after all. If word gets out that he's been spying on the terra-cotta priests, it could ruin him."

"You were worried I would let it slip, weren't you?" I accused. "That I would say something to the Archduke and get us into trouble."

"That was part of it," Nero admitted. "You are a poor liar, and you hate being lied to. Especially when the person doing it is a noble."

As much as I hated to admit it, Nero was right: I could put on a false face when it suited me, but even the best gamblers have tells—instances in which their facade slips and they overplay their hands—and mine were worse than most.

"But the curse changes all that," Nero continued. "If we are going to navigate this mess, you need to know what everyone stands to gain, or to lose."

"And the Varangian? Whose side is he on?"

"Rurik? Same side as always. His own. The man likes his job, but he has always wanted to die with a blade in his hand on the battlefield, not from some flesh-eating disease in the middle of nowhere. His loyalty is to staying alive, not Adler."

"Why not walk away?"

"Not an option. Besides, it is better for us that he stay. That's why he and I planned that little reunion, so that we would have an excuse to speak alone from time to time. This way, whatever Adler or the Archduke plans, we will know."

"I see," I replied, frowning at the memory of their so-called reunion. "Was the punch some sort of code?"

"Caught that, did you?"

"I know your reaction time nearly as well as I know my own. You had to know the blow was coming, or it would have hit you."

"As long as everyone else bought it, that's fine. He and I had three signals. A salute, a shove, and the punch."

"Let me guess, the more violent the greeting, the deeper we are in shit?"

"More or less." Nero gestured for us to double back. "Anyway, that's everything. Now you know as much as I do."

We walked in companionable silence for a stretch after that. To our left, the sun had already begun to dip behind the hazy peaks of distant mountains, casting the valley in shades of muted gold. In the distance, tents blazed with reflected light as Adler's people worked to turn on the camp's myriad assortment of ventlamps.

"Nero," I said, haltingly, "if the Order finds out what has happened here and demands we withdraw, or worse…"

"Want to know the hardest part about growing old, Valentine? Finding something to care about. Nothing matters like it used to. You spend most of your time watching people you know die. Your family dies. Your friends die."

"What has that got to do—"

"I am not interested in what the Order wants us to do. One of the few friends I have left asked for my help. Curse or no curse, that has not changed."

"I understand."

"But you don't agree."

I shrugged. "I defied the Order once, and people died. A lot of people. I would rather not make that mistake again."

Nero reached out and planted a hand on my shoulder—a gesture far less reassuring than I believe he meant it to be, if only because he was about as doting as an animal that routinely ate its young.

"There's no need to worry," he said. "I will keep your name out of it, should it come to that. And besides, whatever they say, you won't be here to hear."

It took me a moment to realise what Nero meant by that. "Oh, right. My flight to New Rome. Why are you sending me there?"

"Research. Adler claims they have stumbled upon some sort of labyrinthe. The locals had no idea anything was down there, which means it probably predates their ancestors. But that's not nearly enough to go on. What we need right now is information. Anything that might help us figure out what this curse is tied to, or even which culture might have cast it. They are far more likely to have records of such things in Constantinople."

"So we are clear," I said, "you want me to take the first available skyship to New Rome, find some obscure mention of an underground labyrinthe that could have been built at any point in time before this area was settled, and rush back with some crucial tidbit that will help us lift a curse no one knows anything about. Should I bring back souvenirs while I'm at it? Perhaps a chest full of gold, a bottle of Caesarean rum, and some bare-breasted courtesans?"

If Nero was amused, he did not show it.

"I know the odds are long," he replied, instead. "But it's possible Adler will help us narrow down the search once he and the Archduke are done squabbling. Also, if all else fails...you could always track down the exile. Word is he settled there, and you know he'll have answers."

Despite the pleasant temperature, I shivered. "I am sure he will. But at what price?"

Nero waved that away. "Hopefully it won't come to that."

"You know they may die whether I come back with anything useful or not," I observed. "It'll take at least a week to get there and back, and I cannot be sure the men in that tent have that long. In fact, I'd be surprised if some of them last the night."

"Leave that to me."

"Oh? You planning to yell at them until they recover?"

"Why, do you think that would work?"

I still could not tell if Nero was joking.

XI

THE FIND

*I*t was perhaps an hour past sundown, and the four of us—Doktor Adler, the Archduke, Nero, and myself—sat on the floor beneath a velarium that only partially obscured a star-laden sky. Along the canopy, archaic ventlamps of varying strengths had been strung by ironwire, casting indecisive shadows that stretched in multiple directions as an ungainly lad in an ill-fitting kaftan that left his ankles bare bustled about, topping off our tulip-shaped glasses with a citrusy, aromatic tea. Once he had refilled mine, I settled back against my rucksack, tapping my fingers on its swollen leather hide while the two Germani continued the argument they had been having ever since we first retired to this converted yurt.

"I still do not understand why I cannot at least see the artifact," the Archduke reiterated. "Whatever you found is mine by right. Why should I not get to see what my money has bought?"

"We have been over this, Your Grace," Adler replied, his exasperation plain. "We cannot be sure whether the artifact is the source of the curse, or perhaps connected to it in some way that we cannot yet comprehend. It is risky, plain and simple."

"And yet, here you sit, hale and whole after having laid both eyes and hands upon it yourself. And that still does not explain why you refuse to even tell me what it is you have found, other than to laud its value like dangling a carrot from a stick."

"That was not my intention, Your Grace."

"And yet that was the effect."

"I apologise—"

"I do not want an apology. I want to see what you found down there, and I want to see it, now."

"What you want is irrelevant," Adler snapped. The archaeologist took a deep breath, hunched forward, and bridged his fingers together, momentarily giving the beleaguered academic the air of a back-alley cutthroat. "It is not only your needs which concern me, Your Grace. I have to think about everyone here."

Nero cleared his throat.

"If I may interrupt?"

"Yes, of course," the Archduke said, perking up at once. "Herr Nero will settle this matter. After all, he is the true authority on curses."

"On the contrary," Adler interjected, "the Order has no experts in this field. Curses are far too rare, and far too specific. Finding a Purifier who deals solely in curses would be like finding a sailor who knows how to tie only one knot."

Nero and I exchanged glances.

"Is that true?" the Archduke asked.

"The Doktor is correct," Nero lied. "Once again, he seems remarkably well informed. But then, I wonder, does that mean you also know what the Order suggests we do in circumstances such as these?"

Adler shifted uncomfortably.

"So, you do." Nero took a sip of his tea and nodded. "Then you understand how things stand."

"It would be a mistake, Herr Nero. We do not yet know enough to warrant so severe a reaction."

"Enough!" The Archduke pointed at all of us in turn. "I grow tired of these cryptic conversations. Speak plainly from now on, all of you."

"Herr Nero is implying he could shut us down, Your Grace," Adler explained. "He and Herr Valentine are bound by their oaths to do whatever they must to ensure the curse does not spread, even if that means burning this place to the ground."

The Archduke scoffed at that. "Ridiculous. I hold their contracts. They would not dare. My family's money paid for this excavation, which means this is my property to do with as I see fit."

"Not anymore, Archduke," Nero countered. "Until this curse has been dealt with, one way or the other, our claim to this place supersedes yours."

The Archduke opened his mouth to speak, but Nero cut him off with a gesture.

"In any event, I must agree with you. The artifact they found should present no direct threat to us and is a risk we must take, regardless." Nero turned to Adler. "We need to learn everything we can about what we are facing, and for the moment your artifact is the only clue we have. I would ask you to send someone to collect it."

The Archduke stewed in silence as Adler begrudgingly rose to relay Nero's request to a guard by the door. Not that I faulted the nobleman; the senior Purifier had granted his wish, yes, but only after stripping him of his already tenuous authority. Such an abrupt shift in circumstance was bound to prick anyone's pride—especially that of a Habsburg heir.

"It should not take long." Adler rejoined us on the floor. "In the meantime, I would like to propose a minor alteration to your plan, Herr Nero."

Nero raised an eyebrow.

"My daughter," Adler continued. "I would like to send her along to New Rome so she might assist in the search. She is familiar with Constantinople, and her hands have too long been idle here."

"Your daughter?" The Archduke interjected, his frustration momentarily forgotten. "Kissa is here?"

"Who do you think I sent to escort you, Your Grace?" Adler's eyes twinkled with grim amusement. "She told me how very distressed you were by what you saw. I am certain they were cheered by your willingness to witness their plight firsthand."

"The guide." The Archduke flushed. "I had not realised it was her. It has been quite some time since we saw one another."

"Six years this month, if memory serves. How time soars." The archaeologist swung his attention back to Nero like a hooded cobra tracking a new target. "I ask that my daughter be given the same respect you would show me. In fact, think of her as my representative. This way I can be assured that everything that can be done to save my people is being done."

"I do not think that is a good idea, Doktor."

"And I am afraid I must insist. You may indeed have our best interests at heart, Herr Nero, but experience has taught me the value of the adage *vertrauen, aber überprüfen*. To trust, yes, but also to verify."

"That I understand, but it is not what I meant. I think it is a bad idea because Valentine cannot be expected to see to your daughter's safety as well as his own. It could be dangerous."

"Oh? Perhaps I misunderstood. I was under the impression Herr Valentine was hunting answers, not monsters." Adler flashed us both a condescending smile. "Not that it matters, either way. Kissa is more than capable of protecting herself."

Nero shot me a gauging look, to which I could only shrug; if the archaeologist wanted his daughter to tag along this badly, there was little we could do to change his mind. Besides, the woman had already proven herself a credible source of information, and we could use any help we could find.

"Fine," Nero said, at last. "But you'll have to arrange her travel accommodations, yourself."

"I will see she has everything she needs," the Archduke interjected, eagerly.

Adler clapped his hands together. "Excellent. And here comes Rurik, now."

The Varangian ducked beneath the canopy carrying a box swaddled in black cloth and wreathed in chains bound by a single lock. Adler gestured, and Rurik moved to the darkest patch of tent—as far from prying eyes as possible. The archaeologist retrieved a key from his pocket and tossed it to his man. After removing the lock, Rurik unwound the chains, grasped the black sheet by both ends, and flung it off.

Beyond the bars of a steel cage lay a helmet forged in a style not unlike those worn by Greek soldiers many centuries past—with its jagged noseguard, its almond-shaped eye sockets, and its flaring horsehair crest, the helm would have been an exemplary relic of a bygone age if not for one exceptionally notable delineation.

"Holy Caesar," the Archduke whispered, awestruck. "Is that made of what I think it is?"

"Pure gold, Your Grace," Adler confirmed. "Every gram of it. My men found this outside the chamber we were hoping to unearth the day they became ill."

The Archduke's eyes widened. "Do you think there may be more down there?"

"We cannot be certain, Your Grace. But it is possible. The helmet is Corinthian in style, though there are some Thracian influences of note. If pressed, I would estimate its origin as pre-Classical. Ordinarily, I would have sent for an expert and sought confirmation. But, given the implications, not to mention the sickness...well, it did not seem prudent."

"A wise choice, Herr Doktor," the Archduke added, breathily. "Very wise, indeed. We would be foolish to bring in any more outsiders moving forward. We must involve only those we can trust. In fact, I shall send for a few of the men I brought with me to guard this place. We dare not risk something as precious as this excavation site to bandits."

Nero leaned forward. "You forget yourself, Archduke. You are not to send for anyone. Am I understood?"

"Now, Herr Nero, surely you must see why—"

"I do." Nero glanced at the treasure sitting not a dozen paces from us and shook his head. "Believe me, I know what this means for you and your family. But I cannot allow you to put the lives of yet more people at risk."

"That is hardly my intent." The Archduke waved that comment away. "My soldiers would guard the perimeter, nothing more. Besides, I can assure you my people would lay down their lives for me in an instant if that is what I required."

"That is not the point. I forbid it, Archduke."

"Forbid it?" The Archduke picked up his glass and took a sip of what by then had become a lukewarm brew. "Perhaps you misunderstand. I recognise your expertise in this matter, Herr Nero, but I do not recognise your authority. I will do as I wish. If you intend to oppose me, that is your decision, foolish though it would be."

"Perhaps I was not clear before," Nero rasped, anger giving his voice a timbrous hiss. "If I so much as see an unfamiliar face before Valentine returns, I will torch this place and bury that treasure so deep that no one will ever find it, and I'll do it all with the Emperor's blessing."

"We shall see about that," the Archduke replied, darkly. "I find this conversation unpalatable. Herr Doktor, if you will excuse me? I think I shall retire early for the evening. Would you kindly invite Fraulein Adler to join me in the morning? The whistlecoach leaves at dawn."

"Of course, Your Grace."

"Thank you." The Archduke rose, bowed, and had already turned to leave when he laid eyes on me. "I suggest you find me before my man arrives, Herr Valentine. I will not tolerate a delay."

I raised my glass in a silent toast.

"I did try to keep him from seeing the helm," Adler said once the Archduke was out of earshot, his gaze trained on Nero's face. "I knew it would spell trouble, once he did. Perhaps next time you will consult me before you throw me under the whistlecoach."

Nero grunted. "I wouldn't count on it."

"Speaking of whistlecoaches, do you think the Archduke really meant to meet before dawn?" I cut in. "Because I really prefer to wake up later in the day…"

The two men gave me nearly identical looks.

"Nevermind."

XII

CIVILISED CONVERSATION

"*H*err Valentine, is that you? What are you doing here so early?"
Roused by the unexpected address, I sat up, squinted against the sudden glare, and stifled a yawn. The Archduke, immaculately dressed in the muted austerity favoured by the Empire's more hawkish aristocrats, loomed over me with the sickening disposition of a morning person; despite having endured the same overnight flight I had, the nobleman practically vibrated with verve and purpose. Of course, he had whiled away the last two days enjoying the superior comforts of a luxury cabin, whereas I had been relegated to the lesser of the only two compartments still available mere hours before takeoff—a communal sleeper occupied by an Anatolian couple and their colicky infant.

"Your Grace," I replied, groggily, "to what do I owe the pleasure?"

The Archduke did not immediately reply, but rather signaled to a waiter standing against the far wall of the otherwise empty dining room and took the seat across from mine. A glance through the slatted windows that rimmed the ceiling revealed a rising sun that had only just begun to crest the clouds, which meant I had dozed off for no more than half an hour since retiring to this relatively quiet oasis. A shame, considering I could have used several hours more.

"Would you like your usual, Your Grace?" the waiter asked.

"That would be ideal, thank you. One for my friend here, as well. I believe he could use some enlivening."

"Of course, right away, Your Grace."

The waiter departed as unobtrusively as he had arrived—a talent for modesty which I often envied in others. Of course, stature aside, I was not built for subtlety; my face unsettled even the most vapid, and my temperament was such that I would rather cut a stranger than chat with them.

When the waiter returned, he began transferring a series of opulent accoutrements from a copper tray to our table: polished silver cake trays loaded with all manner of glazed puffs and powdered pastries, followed by brass bowls brimming with sugar cubes and melted cocoa; sugar spoons, tongs, and teaspoons laid alongside dessert forks and butter knives; stoke china cups nestled inside pewter bowls placed atop saucers laced with silver filigree. What arrived last, however, was not the steaming pot of tea I had been expecting, but a rather comically large ladle seething with a frothy, russet-colored liquid.

"Anatolian coffee," the Archduke explained as the waiter poured its sludgy contents into our cups. The smell of it permeated the air—an aroma somehow both acrid and appetizing, yet ultimately unfamiliar. "Quite the history, this drink. Would you care to hear it, Herr Valentine?"

"Depends. May I drink while you talk?"

"Of course. Though I would mind my tongue if I were you."

"Hm?" I glanced up, startled by the undercurrent of menace in the Archduke's tone.

The nobleman wore an uncharacteristically predatory smile that had me reflexively reaching for the nearest utensil. By the time I held the dessert knife clenched in my fist, however, the baleful grin was gone—supplanted by the exceedingly agreeable facade with which I was most accustomed.

"The coffee, Herr Valentine. It can get quite hot." The Archduke's heavy-lidded gaze shifted to the knife in my hand. "Oh, forgive me, would you like me to pass the cakes? I rarely indulge, myself, but I can assure you they are to die for."

"No, thank you."

"Are you certain, Herr Valentine?" he asked, his eyes twinkling with grim amusement. "Why else pick up the dessert knife, if not to enjoy the refreshments? Or perhaps it was a subconscious gesture, on your part?"

Uncertain how to respond, I sat back and marveled at the Archduke's blatant attempts to unnerve and intimidate me. Had I done something to prick his pride? Said something to offend his delicate sensibilities? Unable to reconcile either possibility, I turned my attention to the man himself, taking particular note of his bloodless fingers where they gripped the edge of the table and the compulsive bunching of his jaw. It was only then I realised this little demonstration had nothing to do with me.

It was Nero he wanted to lash out at—Nero who had seized control of the excavation site which should have been the Archduke's to do with as he saw fit. Nero who, before sending us away, had privately accused the Archduke of caring more about profits than people. And so, what with the old man both figuratively and literally out of the Archduke's reach, he had come for me: Nero's surrogate. A younger, less imposing victim he could terrorise to his heart's content. His was a bully's calculation—a foregone conclusion between picking on someone his own bloody size or wailing on the weakest runt he could find. Unfortunately for the Archduke, this equation had one monumentally glaring flaw.

Between the two of us, I was the bully.

"I suppose you could call it professional curiosity," I replied after a moment's consideration, running my finger along the knife's slightly abrasive edge. "Comes with the job."

"Oh? I am afraid I do not follow. Please, enlighten me."

I raised the utensil to the light the way a jeweler might inspect a gemstone, twisting the dull blade so that its polished surface reflected the various colors of the room. "I met a man in prison, once. He was Arabian, well-educated—a physician who made the unfortunate mistake of treating a sheik's mistress for a miscarriage. He and I were chained together for a time. They did that: paired the young with the old. It was a clever tactic. The old men were weak, cautious. Broken. They weighed us down, kept us from fighting back, told us to be patient."

"Herr Valentine, I do not see what—"

"By the time we met, the infection that would eventually kill Fahim had already cost him one side of his face. Worms in his brain. Nasty way to go. Before he died, he used to point to other prisoners and tell me things about them. He would raise his good arm like so and tell me how the man working the crank was going to fall dead in a few days' time, or how the woman who brought our food was spending all her coin on booze. When I asked how he knew, can you guess what he said? He told me it was his job to know. He said that it was a physician's curse to see symptoms instead of people."

"Fascinating, Herr Valentine. Though I still cannot see what that—"

"Did you know that pure silver is lighter?" I balanced the knife on my outstretched finger and met the Archduke's eyes. "This knife is plated, which makes it durable. And heavy. Too awkward for throwing, too dull for stabbing. Unless you plunged it into someone's eye, or maybe thrust it through the roof of the mouth from behind the chin. It's all soft tissue back there. And of course, there's the ear canal, which might as well be an open tunnel leading directly to the brain. You would simply shove it in, like this, then jerk it back and forth. Very messy."

The Archduke coughed into his fist to cover his discomfort. "You seem to have given this a great deal of thought, Herr Valentine."

"On the contrary, Your Grace, that was merely conjecture. There are so many ways to kill a man, after all." I replaced the knife and slid a finger along the tines of a nearby fork, touched the lip of the brass bowl, and waved a hand over the contents of the still steaming ladle. "We can be stabbed, bludgeoned to death, burned...our vulnerabilities are endless."

I waited for my point to sink in, holding the Archduke's wary gaze for several seconds before I splayed both hands and shrugged. "Still," I continued, "I expect nothing arrayed on this table is capable of killing anything worth killing."

"You are referring to an infernal, I presume?"

The Archduke's casual use of the term shocked me almost as much as his sudden civility pleased me; all that underlying hostility seemed to have evaporated into thin air over the span of our staring contest, supplanted by something far more solicitous.

"An...old word for their kind," I admitted, "but yes."

"A prohibited word, you mean. I am not naive, Herr Valentine. My family has seen firsthand how the Empire sanitises everything it touches." The Archduke gestured vaguely towards the three-tiered ventlantern hanging from the ceiling, his voice tinged with unexpected bitterness. "We all know what created those creatures. What sustains them."

"Archduke, you may want to keep your voice down," I cautioned, surprised to find myself agreeing with the man I had so recently cowed.

"Yes, you are quite right. You must forgive me, Herr Valentine. I came here looking for an excuse to be angry with you when I should have been thanking you, instead."

"Thanking me?"

"For what you do. For what your Order does. In a way, you are all that protects us from ourselves. That deserves gratitude, not disrespect. Which is why it pains me to say this." The Archduke hunched forward and lowered his voice to a faint whisper. "If your Order ever again tries to manipulate me or anyone else in my family like what happened yesterday, I will have no choice but to devote myself to burning your precious library to the ground."

"I do not—"

"Please, Herr Valentine, do not sully my improved opinion of you with a denial. Your Order does not have a monopoly on information. I know all about the Varangian and what he told you. Though, in truth, I do not care that you know. All that matters to me is that you and Herr Nero do as you have promised. As long as you rid the site of this curse, keep the Archduchess safe, and stay out of my affairs, I am willing to swear on my sister's life this will be the last uncivilised conversation we shall ever have. Am I understood?"

After a moment's consideration, I raised my now lukewarm cup of coffee in a mock salute. "You are understood, Your Grace. To civilised conversation."

"Yes, I like that. To civilised conversation."

I waited until the Archduke tilted his own cup back before taking a wary sip of the tepid beverage. The result was a rich, startlingly bittersweet experience unlike anything I had ever tasted. I braved a second, more ambitious attempt and found my mouth assaulted by brackish sediment that swarmed my tongue and teeth.

"It is an acquired taste," the Archduke noted, plainly amused by my reaction. "As I was saying before, the bean this drink is derived from is both harvested and distributed by the Afrikani. They control every aspect of its production, which allows them to inflate their prices, create artificial shortages, and even exercise leverage in unrelated negotiations. Indeed, some say the Nubian Kingdoms would never have thrived were it not for their stranglehold on this particular good."

"This?" I eyed the liquid suspiciously. "Truly?"

"Indeed, Herr Valentine. That cup alone would cost you a silver deni."

"A silver? For a single cup?"

The Archduke chuckled. "Give it time, and you will understand."

I had only just opened my mouth to ask what the Archduke could possibly mean by that when we were joined by another passenger. Sporting a pair of cowhide gladiator sandals, billowing black trousers, and a crisp, cap-sleeved blouse clasped down the middle with obsidian chips, the woman who sashayed into the room had the dark complexion of a native Anatolian but the auburn tresses and robust features of the notorious tribe of nomadic women known to migrate between the Scythian steppes and the beaches of Thrace—those tempestuous gypsies we call Amazons. Of course, not even her unconventional attire could have upstaged the whorling, indigenous tattoos which swarmed up her right arm and caressed her throat, cheeks, and chin.

"Ah, so Fraulein Adler deigns to join us, at last." The Archduke swirled his coffee with a practiced ease. "I had wondered whether she would accept my invitation."

An enterprising steward moved to intercept, clearly hoping to herd the foreigner to a corner table where she would be considered an oddity and not an eyesore. A minor argument ensued, punctuated by a series of fervent gestures, including an imploring wave aimed in our general direction. The woman scowled as she sought us out, and only then did I genuinely recognise Adler's daughter and chosen representative.

"I believe she meant that for you," the Archduke asserted.

"Yes. Excuse me for a moment, Your Grace." I dabbed at my mouth with a white linen napkin, rose, and strode across the room feeling both a tad flushed and far less lethargic than I had when the Archduke arrived. Indeed, I felt more alert than I had in weeks—a side effect, I later learned, of that delightfully bitter, horrendously expensive brew. "Is there some sort of problem here?"

"Please, forgive the disturbance, Signore. I was merely trying to tell the Signorina—"

"I was actually speaking to the lady," I interjected, making a point to ignore the steward. "The Archduke has been expecting you, Fraulein Adler. May I?"

"You may." Kissa slid her bare arm through mine with practiced ease. "We would not want to keep His Grace waiting any longer than is necessary."

We left the steward standing there with his mouth half open and his hands out as though he planned to forestall us. But of course, he did nothing of the sort. Only a fool would waylay an acquaintance of the Archduke's, even if that acquaintance were in violation of the *Ex Machina*'s ultraconservative dress code.

"I see skyship hospitality has not improved much in the last few years," Kissa muttered, her full-lipped mouth pursed in irritation. "I wish I understood why Auxiliaries like him behave as they do."

"The entitlement, you mean?"

"No. That I understand, already. He is a man, not to mention an honorary citizen of an Empire that spans half the known world. Men like that wear their pride like they wear their skin. What I cannot grasp is why the unfamiliar offends them so much."

"Offends whom?" the Archduke asked, having caught the tail end of Kissa's comment. The nobleman had already risen and pulled out a chair for our guest, his posture almost caricaturish in its smarminess. "No one I would associate with, I trust?"

"I cannot speak to the company you keep, Your Grace. But no, I think not. Intolerance was never your vice."

The two met each other's gaze and held it, an unspoken tension flaring up between them that I could neither explain nor comprehend. The Archduke's smile became a brittle thing as he bowed and disengaged, returning to his own chair with all the aplomb of a wounded feline.

"I will have another cup brought, Fraulein Adler. I seem to recall you enjoyed the taste." The Archduke raised a hand as though to hail the waiter, then froze. "Where did the staff go?"

Kissa and I turned as one to find the entire room implausibly vacant. Gone were the two stewards with their patronizing smiles and simpering platitudes, not to mention the half-dozen mild-mannered servers who traditionally loitered in the alcoves, waiting to be summoned. Indeed, all that remained were a half-dozen crockery-laden tray tables and a smattering of strategically placed water pitchers.

"Something is not right," Kissa said, immediately. "Where could they have gone?"

"Maybe they got called away," I ventured.

"All of them? With the Archduke here? I think that unlikely."

"Let us have a look for ourselves," the Archduke suggested. "I am sure we caught them in the middle of a shift change, or some such. There is nothing to worry—"

Before he could finish, however, a deafening alarm began bleating above our heads. I covered my ears, cursing as the sconces on the wall began pulsing with ventlight. Kissa, meanwhile, strode purposefully towards the hallway.

"What is she doing?!" the Archduke yelled, his words barely audible above the blaring sirens.

I shook my head.

"I am going after her!"

The Archduke hurried across the room and had almost caught up to Adler's daughter when the skyship veered violently starboard, tilting so grievously on its axis that the hallway doors momentarily became the ceiling. All three of us were yanked off our feet, and for one brief, faintly exhilarating moment, we hung suspended in midair like marionettes held aloft by invisible strings.

And then, gravity took over.

XIII

INTERLUDE: TRAUMA

*W*hen I was a younger man, I visited a bazaar in Thebes where I, among a crowd of jeering onlookers, gathered to watch a street performer pull dozens of tiles out of a sack that should have held perhaps a quarter that number.

The tiles were hand painted, each representing but a fragment of an image that took shape as he flung them about—a feat that became more and more impressive with every unerring throw. Once the mosaic was complete and his audience satisfied, he pocketed his donations, asked his young assistant to collect the tiles, and began again.

In truth, it was not an inspired performance. Some sleight of hand, a little showmanship, and a flawless memory. Indeed, the only reason it has stuck with me all these years is what happened the one time he failed to produce the image. I can still remember his startled face when he drew the first unfamiliar tile. Apparently a rival had swapped several of them with dubious facsimiles—a prank that left the performer as befuddled as his creation was flawed.

Several years later, back when I was still working alone and before I discovered my true discipline, I killed a Domina who had made a small fortune feeding her wealthiest clients to a pet succubus she kept caged in the wine cellar. She was not a cruel mistress, from what I understand. Her girls were treated well, their needs catered to. But then, that is not particularly surprising. In my experience, even murderers have at least one redeeming quality.

In any case, those few who survived the encounter with the succubus became addicts—slavish fiends willing to trade away their lands, titles, and inheritances for yet another fatal caress. Ironically, it was their dispossessed children and jilted spouses who brought the brothel-keeper's illicit activity to the Order's attention.

I will not trouble you with the details of the Domina's grisly death, but I should note it was ultimately prosaic compared to the bloodbath that was unleashed when her captive succubus broke free during our struggle. I found the grotesque creature mounted atop a headless corpse several hours past sundown, riding his lifeless body like a child's hobby-horse, her scaly flesh coated liberally in the blood of the half-dozen men who had caught her scent and come running only to tear each other apart for the honor of dying inside her.

For some reason, I have always associated that uniquely disturbing, altogether chaotic episode with that failed street performance—struck perhaps by how our minds can take an absurd number of fragments and arrange them in a seemingly logical sequence over and over again, only to falter the moment we encounter a piece that could not possibly fit.

That, I think, is the essence of trauma.

XIV

CALAMITY ON THE OPEN SKIES

 hen the skyship banked, time became an abstract concept devoid of reason or sense. Indeed, much of what I am left with are a jumble of chaotic memories I can only begin to sort through—indiscriminate snippets accompanied by flashes of color and eruptions of sound. The sugar bowl which arced across the room like some copper comet, for instance, or the toppled tower of lacquered charger plates rolling across the floor like the spilled contents of a coin purse.

And then, of course, there are the bits I might very well have imagined, like the jet-black flower petals emerging from the inky tusks of the tribal boar tattooed on Kissa's shoulder as she tumbled past, or a streak of Imperial red from the lining of the Archduke's otherwise drab doublet vanishing behind the voluminous folds of a round linen tablecloth while the table it belonged to—having been bolted down in anticipation of just such an occasion—stayed right where it was.

Piecing it all together from the subsequent aches and bruises, I can say with a reasonable amount of certainty that my own chair took me out at the knees as it fell, at which point I was flung forward onto my face and forced to scrabble in vain while I slid across the slick cork floor, bouncing off bolted-down furniture. Eventually, I slammed up against something firm and unyielding—a blow which drove the breath from my battered lungs.

Overhead, the ventlantern swung wildly on its chain, its wrought iron frame tearing hideous gouges in the painted ceiling while beams of sunlight shone through one window after the next, wheeling furiously as the skyship struggled to right itself. I gritted my teeth and tried to get my bearings, praying the *Ex Machina*'s crew would shortly regain control of the unwieldy vessel—that they, at least, were prepared for this. Unfortunately, the turbulence was more than I could handle. My stomach lurched, and I had no choice but to shut my eyes lest I throw up a silver deni's worth of coffee and make the situation that much worse.

What felt like hours passed before the skyship at last lumbered upright, heralded by the muting of the sirens and the dimming of the wall sconces. I sagged to the floor, struggling to breathe. To think. Nothing hurt, yet, though I knew it would in a few hours' time. But I could at least wiggle my fingers and toes, which boded well.

"What the bloody hell was that?" I groaned.

"Herr Valentine? Is that you?"

Dimly, I recognised Kissa's voice, though both her husky contralto and my own baritone sounded oddly muffled, even distorted, to my ear. I reached up, grazing the canal, and my fingers came away slick with blood— never a good sign.

"Here!" I called. "I am over here."

"Are you hurt?"

"The tribunal is still out on that," I replied. "You?"

"Nothing too terrible, fortunately. Hold on, I am coming to you."

Movement on my peripheral suggested the Amazon was on her way. Determined to look a little less pathetic before she arrived, I rolled gingerly onto my side and propped myself up on one elbow. A quick survey of the room revealed a mound of debris piled high against the wall, including the crumpled form of the unresponsive Archduke tucked away beneath a stack of overturned chairs.

"Your Grace?" I called.

When the Archduke failed to so much as twitch, I braced myself to rise and check his pulse. I had managed to get to all fours, in fact, when a new voice thundered through the room.

"Right, men. Let's get them up. Restrain those two and stash them with Flynt on the lower decks. And stay on your guard! We cannot afford another setback. The rest of you, take care of the staff in the hallway."

A chorus of affirmatives echoed in the wake of that perplexing speech.

Perhaps a dozen black clad figures in familiar finery surged into the room to collect us, tugging and supporting in equal measure until we were all more or less upright.

A stolen glance to my left revealed a disheveled but ultimately hale Kissa struggling to fend off three men as they bound her wrists. The Archduke, meanwhile, lay limp in the beefy arms of the largest captor, bleeding profusely from a shallow gash above one eye. Before I could even consider putting up a fight of my own, two of the men yanked my arms behind my back and tied my wrists together with a remarkably coarse rope. A sudden bout of pain and nausea ripped through me, and I ended up heaving all over the shoes of the man on my right.

"Disgusting," he said.

"You better not ride down with us," his companion said, taking my other arm. "You will stink up the lift."

Sadly, no one seemed to care about my discomfort or the sorry state of the floor.

"Well done," their leader said once Kissa was secured. The man stood with his back turned towards all of us so that all I saw of his face was a quarter profile and the cultivated curl of a waxed moustache. "Now, let's move, Mercantiles. This skyship is not going to steal itself."

A.D. XI KAL. APR. MMCDLIII A.U.C.

APRIL 2ND, 1770

Carcer on the Outskirts of Cappadocia

Malum consilium quod mutari non potest.

It is a bad plan that cannot change.

PEOPLE

OF THE ERA

I

INTERLUDE: AFTERMATH

The sandstorm my cellmate predicted has come and gone, leaving the uneven floor of my dingy cell carpeted in a layer of carmine grit so thick it has stained my ankles a ruddy shade of brown and caked my feet in an ochre clay. Though the last crack of thunder sounded over an hour ago, the sky-searing foetor of burning ozone continues to fester in the air, making my teeth ache and my eyes water—a side effect, one must presume, of the various toxins and pollutants whipped up by the these terrible, rainless storms.

My neighbour has fallen mute once more and refuses to speak to me despite the fact our jailers have yet to return from the tunnels below the city. I cannot say what is taking them so long except to speculate they were needed elsewhere. Perhaps sweeping the city clean of dust and debris is a compulsory activity required of every Cappadocian citizen, or perhaps they snuck off to slake their thirst while no one would think to look for them.

For their sake, I hope it is the latter.

Outside, the warbling song of the spiked magicians has begun in earnest. Soon, the night shift will arrive with their ventlamps and idle chatter—a welcome respite from the cheerless ennui that accompanies the darkness. Until then, I will persevere with what little daylight I have left and pray the food they bring is more palatable than what I have been treated to thus far.

I do not have high expectations.

II

CAPTIVE

*O*ur captors split up into two groups as we exited the dining room, one of which herded Kissa and me towards the gear-encrusted doors of the nearby skylift while the other—spearheaded by the brutish goon who cradled the Archduke in a way that reminded me of that ridiculous painting of Tiberius surrounded by the penitent crowds at Calvary with the lifeless body of the Nazarene in his arms—made for the stairs.

In a bid to buy time, I doubled over and feigned another bout of nausea. One of the Mercantiles wrenched me upright with one tear-jerking tug of my hair.

"Move," he barked, shoving me forward. "You do not want me to have to tell you twice."

I clenched my teeth but did as he asked, swallowing the blatant contempt I have always held for thugs. There was simply nothing I could do. Besides, we had bigger concerns at the moment. Like what had caused the *Ex Machina* to spin out of control, and what did they want with the Archduke? For that matter, what did they want with us?

And, perhaps most perplexing of all, what could these blithering idiots possibly want with a skyship?

I simply could not make sense of it. Unlike caravans and seafaring vessels, skyships were notorious for being immune to the hazards of buccaneers and brigands. It was, in fact, a rather large part of their appeal.

There were several reasons for this, though only two which actually mattered. The first was logistical—a question of getting off a skyship once it was airborne without plummeting to one's death. The second, of course, was philosophical—what good was coin in the hands of a corpse, which is what you would undoubtedly become should you make an enemy of those who owned the bloody skies?

Even assuming you could somehow account for the former, to blatantly disregard the latter was, well, let me just say that this scheme—whatever it might have been—smacked of suicidal intent.

The skylift doors ratcheted open before I could dwell on these questions any further, revealing yet another Merc with one hand on the crank and the other on the brake lever. While he worked to stabilise the bulky transport, Kissa and I were summarily shoved inside, thrust up against the walls, and instructed to neither move nor speak.

"Take us down."

The skylift operator did as he was told, at which point it finally occurred to me why these men had looked so familiar before: they were clothed head to toe in the uniforms worn by senior stewards, complete with shining black leather boots, black trousers, double-breasted waistcoats, and diamond cufflinks—each of which, I might add, cost more than a Nester whore could earn in a year.

Of course, that was where the similarities ended; the average age of a senior steward typically landed somewhere between fogey and fossil. Combine that with the sheer improbability of seeing more than one senior steward on any given ship at any given time, and I could only conclude reputation alone had shielded these men from the scrutiny which might have exposed the ruse—including routine queries like "what do you think you are doing on this deck?" or "why are you pulling that lever?" or "where are you taking that body?"

Coincidentally, you should know there are very few satisfying answers to that last question—none of which include the phrase "to do with as I please."

Do with that what you will.

III

THE COPPER CARTS

*W*hat I assumed would be a swift descent to the lower decks became instead a time-consuming, tiresome affair plagued with stops. On nearly every floor, black clad figures armed with sabers and pistols roamed the corridors, ransacking compartments and harassing civilians. Many of our captors joined them, trickling out in twos and threes until we left the middle decks behind, at which point all but a handful remained.

Had I been a more accomplished pugilist, I might have made a move, then. Snapped my head back into the nose of the bastard breathing down my neck, perhaps, or delivered a knee to the nearest groin. Unfortunately, I had neither the strength nor the skill to best any of them with a single blow, especially with both arms bound behind my back. What I needed was my blade or, better yet, my scissor—both of which were, to my great frustration, stored in the *Ex Machina*'s reputedly impregnable vaults.

In any case, the opportunity was lost once we reached our destination—a floor just above the one I had left behind but a few short hours ago.

The lower-class compartments, commonly referred to as "copper carts" thanks largely to their cheap ticket costs and inferior comforts, were stuffed with over a hundred squatting passengers, many of whom had spilled out into the corridor to treat the various injuries inflicted during the skyship's midair maneuver.

Indeed, the scene itself was far more what one might expect from the triage wing of an understaffed hospital than the furnished halls of a luxury aircraft. Here and there, traumatised children clutched at their parents—some sobbing, others pale and glassy-eyed with shock. Worse still were the neglected babes, their minders either too stunned or too hurt to stifle the ceaseless wailing. And then there were the architects of this woeful affair: a small platoon of saber-wielding Mercantiles hovering like vultures, several of whom were armed with double-barreled dragoons.

As we were shoved out into the hallway, a portly fellow with bloodstains up to his elbows huffed to his feet, complaining that his patients needed proper medical attention. To condemn them to a slow death when they could be saved was a travesty, he insisted—a deplorable and inhumane act that would earn the Mercantiles no leniency when they were eventually caught. A dozen or so passengers raised their heads, their expressions hopeful.

A sinister-looking Merc afflicted with a substantial hunchback wandered over, his sloped face dominated by a singularly large, bright blue eye. Once within striking distance, he backhanded the physician with all the consideration one might reserve for a buzzing insect—a vicious blow which sent the poor sod careening into a mother and her two children. Startled cries rippled throughout the corridor, echoed by terrified children.

"We do not question how you do your job, leecher," the hunchback said, his oddly melodic voice carrying above the din. "So do not question how we do ours. Now, as for the rest of you! I believe you were told to shut up and keep still, were you not?"

The cries died out as the majority of passengers ducked their heads like scolded dogs. Children's mouths were swiftly covered while mothers rocked their squalling babes. I was not surprised; the lower decks were filled with ordinary, working-class folk all too familiar with the bit parts they were meant to play in situations like these.

"That's better," the hunchback continued. "Now, if you have to bleed out to keep quiet, then that is what you will do. Do not bother us again, or I swear I will personally throw the next halfwit to speak out of turn into this bloated contraption's cesspit and leave them to drown in a vat of shit and piss."

The colourful threat seemed to cow the rest, and a pall fell over the hall-way, interrupted only by the sound of the clanking machinery beneath our feet and the sound of the hunchback's laboured breathing as he turned towards us.

"What are you all doing down here?" he called.

"We found these two on the upper decks. Boss said to leave them with you."

The hunchback, who presumably went by the name Flynt, grumbled something inaudible under his breath and bid us forward. Our captors carved a path through the terrified passengers, presenting us to the man like human chattel—a reality I could speak to with some measure of authority. Flynt gestured to our bound wrists.

"Why the ropes?"

"Boss insisted."

"They put up a fight?"

"This one did." A Merc grabbed a fistful of the Amazon's hair and tugged her head back, causing her to grimace and hiss. "But we dealt with her."

Flynt scowled. "And what about him?"

The same Merc barked a laugh. "He threw up all over Paulo's shoes. Probably would have started crying, too, if we'd let him."

I slumped my shoulders and averted my eyes as though stung by the jibe —aping the posture of a man who has been knocked low so many times he no longer bothers to rise. Better they think me a spineless ponce, I decided, than a threat.

"Anyway," the Merc continued, glancing back at the gaping skylift doors, "they're your problem, now."

"You in a rush?" Flynt growled.

"The men upstairs will want to be relieved, soon. We agreed to take turns keeping an eye on the first mate and the new pilot after the old one tried to back out on our deal."

"So, that's what happened."

"Aye. The Boss killed him. The Captain, too."

"Probably for the best. And the rest? Is everything else going according to the Boss' plan?"

"Seems like it, but you would have to ask him. I'm just the errand boy. So? Are we good to leave these two with you?"

Rather than reply right away, Flynt fixed each of us in turn with the belligerent stare of a man who has lost everything there is to lose but his spite—the nasty, pugnacious sort you instinctively avoid in public and should never be alone with in private.

"Are either of you going to cause me any trouble?" he asked.

"No, Signore," I replied, averting my eyes. "We would not dream of it."

From the look on Kissa's face, I thought the Amazon might lash out and condemn us both to yet another beating, or worse. But then she, too, looked away. She shook her head.

"No, Signore. No trouble."

"Good." Flynt swung the barrel of his dragoon about and used it to point to the far end of the hallway, oblivious to those passengers who squealed and scampered to get out of his line of fire. "Put them in the corner. But leave the ropes."

IV

WHISPERS & SHOUTS

*T*he displaced passengers quickly poured into the gap our captors left behind, free to resume their paltry roles in our little drama. Mothers and fathers clung to their children, couples clung to each other, and the rest clung to hope. All, however, gave us a wide berth. We were trouble, and had the restraints to prove it.

"At least we won't be overheard," I muttered under my breath.

"What did you say?" Kissa asked, her query barely audible above the steady hum of churning machinery that permeated the lower decks.

"Nothing. Thinking out loud. Are you alright?"

"A few bumps and bruises. And you?"

"Brain damage. Probably going to faint and die any minute now."

"Shame," Kissa replied. "My opinion of you was actually improving."

"Really?"

"Marginally."

"You know what, I think I am starting to feel better."

"Oh?"

"Marginally."

Kissa turned her laugh into a cough as a Mercantile walked past, scanning the crowd with one hand on the hilt of his saber. The others milled aimlessly, their very presence threat enough to quell the passengers. Only the hunchback, Flynt, remained stationary. The others came to him one at a time, huddling for a moment before resuming their patrol.

I shook my head. "The more I see, the less sense any of this makes."

"You are wondering why they would risk their lives to do this?" Kissa asked.

"It's like they must have a death wish. Except none of them seem the least bit scared. And they should be."

"The Five Families," Kissa said, nodding. "They will not let this stand. They cannot afford to. They will have no choice but to make examples of these Mercantiles."

"Exactly. And that's another thing I do not understand. I've encountered Mercantiles before. Theirs is an ideology, not an organization. Mercs may all believe in a commerce-driven society, but they rarely agree on anything else. They don't have ranks, or a command structure of any kind, really. But these men act like trained professionals. They follow orders."

"Perhaps they are mercenaries, employed by Mercantiles?"

"Maybe. But why announce it? No sane person would take credit for this. It will paint targets on the back of every Mercantile from here to the Iron Colonies."

"Perhaps that is your answer. What if it is not Mercantiles, but someone hoping to incriminate them?"

"That would make a great deal more sense," I acknowledged. "It would have to be a wealthy someone, or several someones. We are talking how much it would cost to field a small army. Maybe more. Who could do that?"

"The list is short. The Emperor. The Great Khan in the East, or perhaps one of his sons. The Nubians. The Five Families, themselves. And, of course, your Order."

I scoffed at that. "We are not that wealthy, I promise you. If we were, I would have taken the Archduke's cabin as opposed to a copper cart."

"You stayed down here?"

"A few floors down, I think. It was the best they had available on such short notice."

"Besides the compartment I took, you mean."

I shrugged. "I have slept in worse places. Anyway, the Order has nothing to do with this."

"There is another possibility," Kissa said. "How much do you know about this skyship?"

"Only what I know about skyships in general. Trivia, mostly. I was obsessed with them when I was younger. I was convinced they were going to fall from the sky and kill us all. But about this one in particular, there is not much I can tell you. She's a first-generation flagship, but in better condition than most her age. The *Deus Ex Machina*. That's what the Imperials call her. Rather on the nose, if you ask me."

"How so?"

"The name," I explained. "It's from their plays. It's what they call the device that miraculously solves all the story's seemingly unsolvable problems. The god in the machine. That's what the Florentine's think of their skyships. Floating miracles."

Kissa arched an eyebrow at my derisive tone. "Clearly you do not agree."

"Nothing that costs so many lives to fuel should be considered an act of God."

The Amazon frowned. "You are referring to the mines?"

"Where I'm from, they are called the Vents, but yes. And the ones the Five Families use are reputedly some of the worst in the Empire." I shook my head in disgust. "I cannot even imagine how much infernite a luxury craft like this burns through in a day."

"And which family owns this particular skyship? Do you know?"

"Feretti. It's his family symbol over there on the wall. And on the towels. And the pillowcases."

A look passed across the Amazon's face.

"What is it?" I asked.

"I have heard the name before. Giacomo Feretti. My father mentioned him, once. Rumour has it he is a very ruthless man. A schemer, with ties to the old Pontifex."

"You would know better than I."

Kissa nodded. "Men like that tend to make powerful enemies, and the Five are notorious for infighting behind closed doors. Perhaps this time they have invited the world to watch."

"You think one of the other families might be targeting Feretti, specifically?"

"Or more than one."

"I suppose you could be right," I admitted. "Though none of that accounts for the one thing I truly cannot make sense of."

"And what is that?"

"Their reaction to you."

Kissa blinked, startled. "To me?"

"It is not often an Amazon is spotted this side of the Mare Nostrum, I will grant you, but someone should have commented on your tattoos by now. Instead, it's like they are pretending not to notice what, or how rare, you are."

"How rare, indeed."

I glanced over to find Kissa staring straight ahead, her placid expression belying the underlying hostility in her tone. An ugly bruise had begun to blossom on that side of her face, muddling the intricate tattoo that jutted across her cheek.

"Did I say something wrong?"

"Rare is what you call a reclusive bird or an animal that has been hunted to extinction, Herr Valentine, not a human being."

"That's not what I meant."

"Then choose your words more carefully. Or, better still, do not speak at all. Especially of that which you do not know."

Rather than getting drawn into an argument with such underwhelming stakes, I shrugged and leaned my head back against the wall to stare at the ceiling. Not too far away, I could hear that huffing physician consoling a child with a dislocated arm. The boy's cries were partially muffled by the rope between his teeth.

It was a bold choice, I thought, to continue treating passengers after what Flynt had threatened to do. Foolish, perhaps, but bold all the same.

Kissa nudged me, her face expectant.

"Hmm? Did you say something?"

"I asked how the Archduke looked to you. I was too busy fighting to see for myself. Was he alive?"

"He was unconscious with a cut above his eye, but yes, alive. I think the Mercs, or whoever they are, recognised him for who he is."

"That is not surprising. His face must be on half his country's currency by now. The Dowager Duchess has made sure of it."

"His country?"

"What?"

"You said his country. Not your country."

Kissa shook her head. "It was never mine."

"Understood. Regardless, I wouldn't be too concerned. I wager the Archduke is being treated at least as well as we are, if not better."

"As long as he is alive, it does not matter. Even as a boy, Joseph knew how to hide the parts of himself he did not want others to see. He will have already cozied up to whoever leads these men, I am sure of it. Courting authority is in his nature. That much will not have changed."

"You say that like it is a bad thing."

"It is a survivor's trait," the Amazon replied, shrugging. "There is nothing inherently wrong with wanting to stay alive, just as there is nothing inherently noble in choosing to die. The balance between right or wrong depends on the scale one uses, not the weights themselves."

"Well said."

"I am sorry, Herr Valentine," Kissa said after a few moment's silence. "It was kind of you to offer sympathy, and unfair of me to be so critical. I do not enjoy reflecting on the past."

"I understand that. Better than most, I should think. And please, just Valentine. I prefer the way you say it far more than how Nero does."

"Yes, of course. Valentine. Actually, I had hoped to ask you about that—"

A cry—louder and higher in pitch than those I had grown accustomed to —cut through the din, derailing whatever the Amazon had been about to say. Everyone turned towards the sound to find a man writhing on the floor. It was the physician, I realised, and he was having some sort of seizure. Not five paces away, the boy whose arm he had been popping back into place clutched at his distraught mother.

"What the hell is going on down there?"

Flynt cleared a path as he stumped down the corridor towards our end of the hall, sweeping his pistol to and fro like a blind man with a cane. When he caught sight of the twitching physician, he cursed and scanned the upturned faces gathered nearby.

"Well? Does anyone know how to make this fool stop?" When no one spoke, the hunchback holstered his dragoon and drew a knife from his waistcoat. "Fine. I'll take care of this myself, then."

"Wait!"

I heard my own voice before I even realised I had spoken. To this day, I cannot tell you why I intervened, except to say I could find no merit in watching a man who had risked his own well-being to comfort a crying child get his throat slit without reason.

I may be a Barbari, but I am not a barbarian.

"Who said that?" Flynt demanded.

Several passengers turned to look in my general direction, but none were able to pinpoint who had spoken. Kissa jabbed me with her elbow.

"What do you think you are doing?"

"Getting these ropes off."

"You cannot be serious." The Amazon leaned in so close I could feel her breath on my neck. "What happens when that man dies because you do not have the faintest clue what you are doing?"

"Whoever it was," Flynt bellowed, "better speak up! Or once I'm done gutting this fish, I'm going to find and do the same to you."

"Over here, Signore," I called, ignoring both Kissa's question and her glare. "I can treat him, if you will free my hands."

"You?" Flynt raised his knife and pointed it at me. "You don't look like a physician."

"I am not one, Signore. I am an undertaker from Londinium. My name is Garza."

"A blackmaster?" Flynt scoffed a laugh. "Wait your turn. You can have him once I'm done."

"You misunderstand me, Signore. I can save that man, if you would allow me. I have seen his affliction before."

I ducked my chin and made a point to look as harmless as possible, though I doubted he would need much convincing. I was sleep-deprived, quite possibly bleeding into my brain, tied up, and leaner than a three-legged stray—a corpse might have appeared more threatening than me, were you to stand us side-by-side.

"He is coming," Kissa hissed under her breath. "I hope you know what you are doing."

"No one is going to die. Trust me."

"You had best be—"

The hunchback's shadow fell across us both before Kissa could finish. He lifted his blade a second time, jabbing at the air as he spoke. "I'll cut you loose, but I will be keeping an eye on you. If you try anything, I swear I will gut you, myself. Then I'll do her. That way, you can watch each other bleed out. How does that sound?"

"I...not good?"

"Then try not to disappoint me." Flynt hunkered down and began hacking at the rope the way you might lop off a tree limb. I clenched my teeth and drew the rope as taut as I could, anxious should the bastard miss his mark and slice my hand open. Indeed, it felt as though the rope and my nerves were fraying at an alarmingly similar pace. Thankfully, it snapped before I did.

"Thank you, Signore." I rolled my aching shoulders and wrung my hands together to improve blood flow, glad to be free at last regardless of circumstance or condition.

"You're welcome." Flynt rose to his feet with a disarming smile on his face. "Oh, and if the physician dies? So do you. Good luck."

V

INTERLUDE: AMPUTATIONS

I used the first bonesaw I ever held to decapitate a ghoul. With the second, I cut off a man's leg. His name was Dida, and he was my very first patient. Dida was an affable, cheery fellow, especially for a Thracian pirate. Indeed, I find it hard to think of the man without picturing his easy smile, to recall his voice without hearing his giddy, braying laugh.

Of course, he was also reckless. I remember the Thracian used to sneak out in his nightshirt during unexpected squalls while the rest of the superstitious crew crammed below decks and cursed everything from sea gods to the last woman they laid eyes on. I used to sit on the cabin floor hugging my knees to my chest while those storms raged, my stomach sloshing about like the contents of a cracked cask as I listened to the howl of the wind and the occasional burst of Dida's hysterical laughter.

He was not laughing when the ship's cutter, a Scythian Moor named Stalcast, passed me the saw—though calling it that always felt like equating a switch to a sabre. Indeed, compared to the elegant Medici instrument, Stalcast's preferred surgical implement—a braided wire no thicker than fishing line strung between a pair of handles with hooks on either end—felt like a crude and unwieldy tool in my adolescent hands.

Fortunately, I had seen the thing used often enough to know that once Stalcast placed the wire above the wound, he and I were meant to take up either end and work the handles back and forth until those jagged metal teeth hit the operating table—sawing straight through every last inch of flesh, muscle, ligament, and bone on the way down. Of course, the gap between seeing and doing in this instance was exceptionally cavernous.

"You sure you want my help?" I asked, my native accent perhaps only slightly improved after a year spent surrounded by foul-mouthed pirates.

"It isn't about what I want. Rhesus went back home for a few months, and I need the extra hands. Now, stop dawdling and get on that side of the table, boy. We have at least three more swabbies to work on before the day is through."

"Aren't we going to bleed him, first?"

"Don't be chowder-headed. Bloodletting is not medicine. It's torture, and a slow death besides."

"But I thought—"

"Don't do that."

"But then how—"

"You ask a lot of questions, boy." Stalcast inspected the rag wound tight around Dida's thigh, testing the knot's integrity with his stubby fingers though he need not have bothered. The flesh below the tourniquet was mottled purple from the lack of blood flow. "Tell me this. If we are so much better off without the stuff, then why not bleed ourselves dry right here? Or perhaps you were hoping I'd stab you full of more holes than a salt whore would let you use with your tiny cock?"

I rolled my eyes. "How's come leechers do it all the time, then?"

"Because even a wenching drunk is sober once a day."

"Huh?"

"They get lucky, boy. Sometimes patients live when they should have died, and sometimes they die when they should have lived. A leecher makes his coin by taking credit for the first and blaming others for the second."

"But that's a scam, innit? Why would people pay 'em if that's true?"

"Because real medicine is damned expensive, and the poor can only afford so much. It's peace of mind they buy when they see a leecher, pure and simple. Now, no more questions. We have a job to do."

"That's alright, Stal," Dida chimed in, his ordinarily comely face both flushed and sallow depending where one looked. "The boy was stalling to give me time to finish this bottle. Isn't that right, lad?"

"Quit making excuses for him," Stalcast grumbled. "And I don't want to hear any more from you either, Dida. Drink up. That's all you get to numb the pain, so you best make it count."

Dida did as ordered, tossing back the contents of his grimy amber bottle —a swill so foul I got lightheaded from the scent alone. Once finished, the pirate made a show of toasting us both, his customary grin replaced by a revolted grimace.

"Good lad," Stalcast said. "Now, boy, step back. Stop there. Now, listen closely. I want you to hold tight to your end, and whatever you do, don't let go. You and I will pull it back and forth. No, angle it down. Better. Focus on the motion. Ignore what you hear, ignore what you feel, and don't even think about looking at the leg."

The instant he said it, I found my eyes drawn to the mangled limb. At first, I was unable to make sense of what I was seeing—it all looked like so much raw meat. And then, like some distant landmass coming into focus, it became clear. The pirate's foot hung from his ankle by a strip of tissue so thin that it could tear at any moment. The leg, somehow, was even worse. Mutilated and splintered from having gotten caught between our ship and the one we had attempted to board, what lay before me looked less like a limb and more like a cat that had been ripped apart and dissected by sadistic children.

"Boy!" Stalcast slammed a bloody palm down on the operating table, startling me.

As if on cue, Dida's arm went limp and the bottle slipped from his fingertips to shatter against the deck. The pirate had already passed out— though from blood loss or from tossing back that noxious concoction, I could not tell.

"Caesar damn us all," Stalcast hissed. "Put that rope between his teeth. Go on. Now, remember what I said. Don't look, and do not let go. Are you ready?"

I was not.

But I did it, anyway.

VI

PROMISES MADE

"*E*veryone get back."

The physician lay still when I reached him, his body unbelievably rigid. With effort, I flipped him onto his side and inspected his body for wounds. Unfortunately, it was hard to tell with so much of his body covered in the blood of other passengers. Rather than waste time fretting over it, I began tossing aside anything he might hurt himself on, all too aware that another seizure could overtake the man at any moment if he did not wake up soon.

"Is he going to be alright?"

I turned to find the boy with the dislocated arm staring at me with red-rimmed eyes. His mother still held her hand to her mouth—shock written clear as day across her face. I suppose I could have spared the child's feelings and lied. Many would have. But then, were our positions reversed, I would have wanted the truth.

"I do not know," I replied. "You see how stiff he is? When that happens, it means he is likely to have another fit. It may be as bad as before, or it may not. Only time will tell."

"Is he hurt because he fell?"

"No, he probably hit his head earlier, which can cause this, sometimes. If he does not wake up soon, I may have to hurt him to help him. Do you know what I mean by that?"

The boy sniffed and nodded. "Like my arm."

"Exactly like that. If that happens, your mum will take you to sit with the others over there. Right, Signora?" I glanced up at his catatonic mother and snapped my fingers at her. "Signora, did you hear me?"

"Mamma?" The boy clutched at her sleeve. "Mamma, are you hurt, too?"

The woman jerked, blinking rapidly. After several rapid blinks, she nodded and offered some small reassurance by patting her son's head. I flashed them both the most comforting smile I could manage before turning my attention back to my patient. It was funny. Decades later, I could still hear Stalcast's voice in my head—his stringent lessons as ingrained in me as any I have been taught since.

"If you ever see a man flopping on the deck like a fish," the voice said, "you have two choices. The first is to roll them over like you would a sleeping drunk. Remove anything in reach and wait until the fits stop. If they don't, that leaves you with the second choice."

"To pray," I muttered under my breath. Of course, that was the trouble with relying on the decades' old advice of a middle-aged pirate whose surgical expertise amounted to nothing but triage: if it could not be lopped off, cauterised, or weathered, faith was the only medicine he could prescribe.

Fortunately, I had spent several of the intervening years studying under physicians and scholars—learned men who scoffed at the panacea of prayer until they, too, came up against a disease they could not combat. Unfortunately, everything I had learned since pointed to one ineluctable fact: if this poor bastard kept seizing, I was going to have to cut open his skull.

VII

PROMISES BROKEN

The physician made a better corpse than most. On his back with his arms folded and eyelids closed, he might have been sleeping—something people say far more often about the dead than is actually the case. In a matter of hours, however, he would be like all the rest. Nothing more than a jumble of rotting organs swathed in gray flesh, destined to rot. Already the stink had begun to waft up from his soiled trousers, mingling with the hallway's other odors—the heady musk of perspiration undercut by the fragrance of mink oil and burnsand.

"I told you what would happen if you let him die, blackmaster."

I felt the barrel of Flynt's dragoon settle against the nape of my neck, its cool metal caress sending a shiver up my spine. From this distance, there would be nothing left of my throat once he pulled the trigger; though woefully inaccurate, I had seen firsthand what the pistols were capable of at close range—the fist-sized holes they punched through men's chests left a rather lasting impression.

"And I told you what would happen if we did nothing!" I snarled, dispensing with propriety altogether. "Had you given me what I asked for, I could have saved him."

"Now, now, blackmaster. It's too late to make excuses. Besides, you had to know I was never going to willingly hand you a blade. Still, I'm not an unmerciful man. Executing you would only frighten these pathetic fools.

And the mess...well, let's agree between the two of us that you did what you could."

The weight of the dragoon vanished.

"I'll have some of my men take the body below before the smell sets in," Flynt continued, glibly. "Your services are no longer required. Go back to your little corner before I change my—"

"Flynt! We have company!"

A shifty-eyed Mercantile at the far end of the corridor pointed to the skylift just as its doors cranked open. Inside stood the hulk of a man who had carried off the Archduke some hours before, only now he wore an engineer's uniform with a leather cap slung low across his brow and a neckerchief over his mouth and nose.

"Ah, looks like our time is up," Flynt said with a flash of his crooked teeth. "Guess this corpse is yours to take care of after all, undertaker."

Before I could ask what the hunchback meant, the other Mercantiles began piling into the skylift, their loaded dragoons discouraging any who got in the way. The hunchback slapped me hard on the back as he trotted off after them—a smarting blow that sent me sprawling forward onto all fours.

Muffled cries and furtive whispers erupted as passengers began to realise they were being left to fend for themselves. Indeed, what would have been a welcome development in and of itself proved too much for their distraught captives; several passengers lurched to their feet, clamouring to know what was happening while still more spilled into the hallway.

They surged towards the skylift as one, mobbing that end of the hall even as its double doors clanged shut. The crowd's frenzy began to escalate, their already frayed nerves giving way to panic and anxiety.

I was doing what I could to avoid being stepped on when a tattooed arm slipped under my own and hoisted me awkwardly to my feet. I turned to find Kissa—no longer bound—tugging at me with an insistence I could not ignore.

"If we want to get out of here, we have to hurry," the Amazon said. "Stop dragging your feet."

"But..." I trailed off and spared a glance for the deceased physician. Thus far, no one had disturbed the body. Indeed, even as the passengers vied for space in the crowded corridor, they avoided stepping too close—as if the spectre of death itself were keeping them at bay. Out of the corner of my eye, I caught sight of that sobbing boy, his face hidden in the folds of his mother's skirt as his shoulders shook.

I may have to hurt him to help him.

My own words mocked me with their hubris. Might I have saved the man had Flynt given me his knife? Maybe. Of course, he might still have died, and Flynt might have blown my head off for trying and failing. There was simply no way to know.

"You deserved better," I said aloud, speaking the closest thing to a prayer I could muster.

We all do, I added silently.

"There is no time for that," Kissa insisted. "We should flee before things turn ugly."

"How?" I asked. "The skylift operator controls who goes up and down, and the stairwell has chains on the doors."

"I found another way off this floor. Come on."

I allowed the Amazon to pull me away, albeit with some reluctance. I was exhausted and aching all over, my thoughts so sluggish that I struggled to successfully plant one foot in front of the other. In fact, I was so worried Kissa planned to fight her way through the crowd that I failed to realise we were headed in the opposite direction until we stood before the sliding glass door of an ordinary compartment.

"What are we doing here?" I asked.

"I saw one of those men go in and out. It looks like any other door, but it leads to some sort of service corridor." Kissa tested the handle. "Locked. Block their view so no one can see us. Good, now give me that sash about your waist."

"My cummerbund?"

"Is that really what you people call that?"

"Yes?"

"Then yes, that."

I shrugged, stripped off the pleated sash, and passed it over. "What do you need it for?"

"Now that I have seen what a poor physician you are, I would rather not cut myself," Kissa muttered as she wound the cummerbund about her arm.

Before I could come up with an appropriate retort, the Amazon punched a hole in the glass with her elbow. While she reached in to disengage the lock, I looked around to be sure no one had noticed her little act of vandalism. Fortunately, the other passengers were too busy screaming at one another and pounding on the skylift doors to care about us.

"Got it." Kissa gestured me inside. "Hurry. We do not want them trampling us."

Once we were both through, Kissa shut the door. The interior was dark, though I could make out enough from the light pouring through the hole in the glass to see that what should have been yet another cabin was in fact a narrow walkway that fed into a single corridor which appeared to run parallel with the one we had left behind.

"So, this is how the stewards get around without being seen," I said, marveling at the ingenuity of creating a private hallway for staff.

"That is not all they do without being seen." Kissa pointed to a small curtain on the wall. We approached it together and pulled it aside to reveal an iron grate beyond which was the interior of a cabin much like the one I had briefly shared with the young Anatolian family.

"There is one of these for every room, I would think," Kissa said, disgusted.

"Of course there is," I replied with a sigh, realizing for the first time that the Five's reticence to make their skyship designs public had as much to do with privacy violations as proprietary concerns. "And now I'll never be able to sleep on a skyship ever again."

"I would not worry about that. I doubt they come here to watch people sleep." Kissa patted my shoulder as she wandered farther down the corridor. "I am sure you will be safe."

"You were wrong before, you know," I said as I stepped away from the wall. "I'm not a poor physician."

Kissa looked away. "I am sorry, that was not—"

"He had bled into his brain. The seizures were symptomatic of his condition, not the condition itself. I only agreed to help him because I thought it might be the other way around. When someone has a history of fits like that, they usually wake up after a few minutes. Disoriented, of course, but fine. Assuming they avoided getting hurt during the seizure itself."

"I thought you said you did it because you wanted free of the ropes?"

"There was too little time to explain, then. But I wanted you to know I did not let that man die. Not on purpose."

"Said like a true Purifier," Kissa replied, cryptically.

"What is that supposed to mean?"

"Nothing. Anyway, we should be safe here long enough to decide what to do next. I think there is a smaller service skylift at the end of this hallway. Perhaps we should use it to go find Joseph?"

No sooner were the words out of her mouth than the telltale grind of a descending skylift sounded, accompanied by a strobing vermillion light not some thirty feet ahead of us. We exchanged alarmed looks.

"We have three choices," I said. "We can either run, fight, or hide. But keep in mind we have no idea how many of them there might be."

The Amazon gave me an eloquent look.

"Fight it is."

VIII

INTERLUDE: PITILESS FIGHTS

*I*f you have never before been in a real fight, you should know they are nothing like the choreographed dances you see performed on a mummer's stage. In real life, every sword stroke is designed to maim or kill. There are no needless flourishes, no such thing as witty banter between blows, and certainly no time for vengeful soliloquies or dramatic monologues.

Instead, there is sweat enough to soak one's brow and blind one's eyes. There is also pain—though less at first than you would think; our minds have a way of dulling the sting of a swollen wrist, of soothing the searing ache of an eye that refuses to open, of blunting the deathly chill that sets in once blade strikes bone.

What our minds cannot shield us from, however, is the aftermath—the pulled ligaments and muscle tears that make it impossible to sit or stand, the broken bones and flesh wounds that leave you limping and feeble for the rest of your days.

Of course, what no one ever tells you is how bloody easy they are to lose. How, no matter the number of pitched battles you have won nor the preparations you have made, you are perpetually one blunder away from having your mouth bloodied and your teeth kicked in. How, in the heat of the moment with your heart in your throat and the sound of your own pulse pounding in your ears like breakers surging against a rocky shoal, a genuine brawl is nothing more than a puppet show in the hands of a whimsical child some might call God.

IX

AMBUSH

*W*e ducked out of sight as the skylift ground to a halt. I hunkered down beside the doors with my back to the wall and waited with bated breath to see how many men would emerge. If more than a handful of armed Mercantiles came pouring out, Kissa and I had agreed to turn ourselves in rather than end up gutshot. Miraculously, however, there were but two.

Seeing what I saw, Kissa struck first, targeting the back of her opponent's knee with a swift kick the instant he stepped out into the hallway. His startled cry echoed down the corridor as I abandoned my hiding spot and leapt onto his companion's back, wrapping both legs around the man's narrow torso while I snaked an arm around his neck.

My attack was not without risks, of course. Were he to have ducked his chin before I secured the choke or had enough wherewithal to yank on the arm hooked up over his head, the Merc might have pried me loose. Instead, he made the classic mistake most do when a foreign object is coiled around their throat: he panicked and wrenched on my sleeve like his life depended on it. But by then, my wiry forearm was firmly entrenched beneath his jaw, pressed against the bulging vein in his throat and cutting off the supply of blood to his brain. He began to wobble on unsteady legs.

And then someone tackled us both from behind.

I lost my grip and went skidding across the floor, banging my hip hard in the process. I groaned as I sat up. My choke victim lay sprawled on all fours, gasping for air, while a third figure—a short, heavyset bastard who must have been hidden behind the other two—climbed to his feet. The lumbering newcomer drew a dagger and came for me like a hunter hoping to end the struggles of a wounded animal.

I kicked him in the testicles.

The Merc hissed in pain, managing somehow not only to stay upright but to come at me a second time, lunging from the side so as to avoid a reunion with my boot. His weight hit me like a runaway whistlecoach, pinning me to the floor. He was clearly the stronger fighter, not to mention better equipped. Indeed, the bastard had me at a significant disadvantage in every category but one: experience.

Which was why, when he got to his knees and reared back to strike, I knew exactly what to do.

The bridge of my hand took the man flush in the throat—a savage strike capable of snapping vocal cords and crushing windpipes. My assailant gagged and reached for his throat, dropping the knife. The blade tumbled and clattered to the floor, missing my stomach by a matter of inches. While he wheezed and coughed, I searched blindly for the dagger.

"I'll...kill...you..." he rasped.

"No." With a surge of satisfaction, I jammed the bastard's own blade between his ribs and twisted. "I don't think you will."

He stiffened as blood ran hot over my hand, but I could not take any chances. I struck again and again, burying the blade over and over in the bulge of his belly until I was liberally bathed in blood. In a matter of seconds, he keeled over, his forehead striking the floor with a wet thwap.

After taking several deep breaths, I bucked my hips and dislodged the bastard. His lifeless corpse flopped over, landing with a resounding thud that was inexplicably echoed by several just like it. Panic surged through me as I realised the danger Kissa must be in. I scrambled to my feet, nearly slipping on the sopping wet floor as I sprinted towards the sound.

To my surprise, I found the Amazon mercilessly bashing my first victim's face against a skylift panel coated red with blood and darker fluids. Seemingly satisfied, she peeled him back by his hair to reveal a flat plain of shattered bones, swollen eyes, and missing teeth where a protruding silhouette had been. The third Mercantile lay out in the hallway with a leg bent in on itself, unconscious. Kissa tossed her victim aside and turned, her entire front splotched red with stains.

"I got a little carried away," she said, plucking disdainfully at her ruined blouse and pawing at her chest. "Shame about this. The blood will never wash out."

I was trying hard not to stare when movement in my periphery stole my attention. Shadows danced further down the hall as a door opened and perhaps a half dozen voices spilled into the corridor, the content of their animated conversation drowned out by the sudden drone of hissing pistons and clanking machinery.

"Damnit," I cursed. "They must be coming up from the bottom decks. We have to go before they find us. We'll take the skylift to the upper floors. There should be somewhere we can hide in the middle decks."

"Um, Valentine? That may not be possible. I think I broke the controls."

Kissa gestured to the panel she had used to bash in a man's brains. Through the half dozen or so cracks that marred its surface, refined infernite oozed outward in bifurcating arcs, spreading from the center like incandescent arterial veins from a neon green heart. I cursed a second time.

"I am sorry. I should have paid more attention to what I was doing."

"Please, the fault is mine, not yours. You did what you had to." I spared a glance at the broken shell of a man at her feet before scanning the corridor. "Hold on, do those look like stairs to you?"

"I cannot tell for sure. They are too far away."

"I think they are. If we hurry, we might make it to them before they spot us."

"Where do you think they lead?"

"Hopefully to a nice, quiet place where we can hide until things calm down."

If not, we were as good as dead.

X

THE BURDEN OF NAMES

*K*issa adjusted her elbow so it no longer pressed against my ribs and stared wistfully at the ceiling as though there were something nostalgic about the water stain spread across it. I wondered if our current circumstances had evoked a pleasant memory of some sort, like playing hide-and-find with her father as a girl or sneaking off with one of her friends. Personally, I could find little to recommend it—but then my recollections of being chased by armed men and forced to hide were the sort that ruined appetites.

"I meant to ask you about your name, before," the Amazon said, breaking the silence that had lain between us, undisturbed, for the past few minutes.

"My name?"

"Valentine. Or is that your title?"

"Bit of both, I suppose." I flexed my hands, loathe to find them coated in the congealed blood that clings to the fine wrinkles of one's skin and burrows beneath the fingernails. "Are you sure now is the best time?"

"Why? Is there something else you would rather be doing?"

I peeked through the thin gap in the doorway of the supply closet we had thrown ourselves into shortly after reaching and ascending the stairs, confirmed there was no new movement outside, and leaned back against a shelving unit loaded with cleaning products and disinfectants. Struck by an idea, I reached overhead to grab a tin with a faded label, twisted its cap, and sniffed at its bitter contents.

"Fair point," I replied, hoarsely. "What was it you wanted to know, exactly?"

"Well, everyone knows a Purifier's title pays tribute to a fallen Emperor. But, were that truly the case, should yours not be Valentinian rather than Valentine?"

"It would, if that were true." I poured a scant splash of the tin's foul liquid onto my blood-soaked palm and rubbed my hands together in an attempt to dissolve the sticky residue. It stung like hell, especially where it came into contact with my own nicks and cuts.

"So, your titles have some other meaning?"

"They do. I'm surprised your father did not explain this to you, though. He clearly knew a great deal about us."

Kissa hunched forward and stared at me with a revolted look on her face. "What is that you are putting on your hands?"

"Some kind of alkaline soap? I'm not sure it is helping, to tell the truth. Why, did you want some?"

"Absolutely not."

"Your loss," I said as I worked the tin's sudsy contents between my knuckles and pulled on the tips of my fingers.

Kissa made a face. "Anyway, my father refuses to discuss things like that with me."

"Really? Why?"

"He has his reasons."

"You know, I am having a hard time deciding if you are being unwittingly cryptic, or if you simply enjoy dodging my questions."

"Bit of both," she replied, mockingly. "So, your title?"

I went on fussing with my hands while I considered my response, debating how much or how little to say on what even the most liberated historians considered a taboo topic. Indeed, it seemed the Amazon had somehow managed to stumble upon the very subject I had steered the Archduke away from before this all madness started—albeit in the most roundabout way possible.

"I will tell you," I said, at last. "But first, I should warn you. A great deal of what I say from this point forward may be considered treasonous, depending who you're talking to. I would not repeat it."

"Treasonous?" Kissa tilted her head. "You mean it."

"I do."

"Now I am even more curious."

"Well, first of all, we Purifiers pay homage to no one, least of all the Emperors of Rome. Our titles are a reflection of the Empire's crimes, not its accomplishments."

"What crimes would those be?"

"The ones the human race pay for every day," I replied, my gaze inexorably drawn to the gap in the doorway where a row of ventlamps sat nestled behind alchemical screens which filtered out that eerie glow and filled the hallway with a fair facsimile of sunlight.

"I meant specifically."

"I'm getting there. Could you pass me that rag?"

The Amazon twisted and reached for a cloth on a nearby shelf, her blood stained blouse riding up to expose a flat stomach riddled with yet more tattoos. She made a show of tugging it back into place before passing me the rag.

I cleared my throat. "Thanks. Now, where was I?"

"Something about crimes against humanity."

"Right. Did you know it was Caligula's civic engineers who first studied infernite?"

"What does that have to do with anything?"

"Humour me."

Kissa frowned, her brow furrowed. "Infernite has been around a great deal longer than that, I should think. I have seen relics made with it from an age before the Persians invaded Greece."

"I said studied, not discovered," I clarified. "The Romans were hardly the first race to mine the stuff, but they were the first to wonder whether it was something more than a precious ore, to see its potential as an energy source —as fuel. In fact, it was one of these engineers who designed the very first ventlamp. A rudimentary version, of course, but still."

"Fascinating," Kissa remarked, wryly.

"That engineer's name was Valentine."

That got her attention.

"Really? I do not believe I have heard of him."

"Few have. Caligula had him killed and his name stripped from the official Imperial records."

"What for?"

"For trying to expose a terrible secret that might very well have upended the Empire. Valentine made a connection, you see, between Caligula's resurrection and the cache of raw infernite stored in the catacombs beneath the palace. He knew what the ore sometimes does to dead flesh. But when Valentine tried to speak out publicly, he was crucified for it. Literally."

"Caligula's resurrection?" The look Kissa gave me was eloquent. "You must be teasing. You cannot mean that old fishmonger's tale."

"I do. And it's true."

Kissa waved that away. "It was an outlandish rumour meant to delegitimise the reign of an unpopular man, nothing more. There is not a historian alive who says otherwise. There is no proof."

Except for those unofficial records we kept in our libraries, I thought but did not say. In fact, in many ways Caligula's rise from the dead was our origin story—the first of many overturned dominoes that led to the foundation of the Order. Unfortunately, that was a far longer, far more complicated conversation.

"What you choose to believe is your business," I said, instead. "I am simply trying to answer your question."

"So, what, you are saying your title is that of a revolutionary?"

"No, you have it backwards. My title is tied to Valentine's crime, not Caligula's."

"I am afraid you lost me."

"Valentine designed the first ventlamp."

Kissa just stared at me.

"He designed the first ventlamp," I reiterated, stressing the words. "Were it not for him, infernite might still be nothing more than a precious stone sought out by treasure hunters. His research and discovery altered the trajectory of our entire world."

Kissa scowled. "And what about your colleague, Nero? What was the crime of the man who succeeded Caligula?"

"I assume you are familiar with the Great Fire that devastated Rome during Emperor Nero's reign?"

"Of course."

"And also that, as a result, infernite became the only source of light and heat anyone would trust?"

"Which is what prompted the Senate to outlaw naked flame and forbid its everyday use, yes. This is something even children are taught."

"And what would you say if I told you Nero's soldiers seized control of every cache of infernite throughout the city mere hours before the Great Fire began? Or that he had several insubordinate senators executed the very night before that vote was cast?"

"I would say you sound like a conspiracist."

"I suppose I do. But that does not change my answer. My title is not an honourific, and neither is Nero's. They are wrongs passed down from one Purifier to the next. Wrongs we hope to one day—"

"Stop talking."

"Excuse—"

Kissa lunged forward and clamped a hand over my mouth. "Listen."

I stilled and strained my ears in time to hear a noise on the other side of the door. The sound of footsteps. Men's voices.

Kissa and I exchanged looks, and—after some hasty adjustments—we both peered into the hall through the slit in the door, our faces practically touching. Outside, two Mercantiles dressed as engineers leaned against the wall, passing a bottle back and forth between them with astounding regularity.

"Feretti's men'll be here soon to take her back," one said, his words only slightly slurred. "We should get to the cargo deck."

"Few more drinks," said the other. "I need the courage. Jumping off a skyship with nothing but a blanket...craziest g'damn thing the Boss has ever come up with, am I right? And for what? We didn't even steal nothin'. D'you see some of the jewels on those women?"

"That wasn't the job. 'Sides, would you want to swim with all that extra weight? Can't spend it if you're dead." The Merc took a swig and laughed. "Maybe you'd go splat, instead. Pearls everywhere. Return 'em to where they belong."

"S'not funny. Y'know I have nightmares about goin' splat."

"Well, get over it. Boss says this'll be the biggest haul, yet. And you owe me some coin, so don't go dying."

"Say, where is the Boss? I haven't seen 'im since we snuck on board."

"You're trying to change the subject."

"Am not." The Mercantile hiccupped. "Just wanted to know where the Boss is, that's all."

"He's dealing with some lordship on the upper decks. Probably working him over real good, findin' out stuff."

"What kinda stuff?"

"I don't know, you idiot," the other said, his voice fading as he tossed the bottle to his companion, turned the corner, and disappeared from sight. "You know, Boss stuff."

"Oh, right. Boss stuff."

The Mercantile went to toss back the rest of the bottle, only to find it empty. He shook it, lolling his tongue as though to catch one last drop, then flung it against the wall. It bounced off and hit the floor without smashing, which only seemed to make the Merc sad. He took off after his companion, complaining about being left behind.

It was not until the sound of their voices faded completely that I realised just how close Kissa and I had ended up to one another; the Amazon sat across my lap, both hands on my chest for balance, her cheek hovering mere inches from my own. I felt her breath across my cheek as we disengaged, both of us moving ever so slowly, our eyes lingering on each other's mouths.

"We should," I coughed, my throat suddenly dry. "We should try to find the Archduke. If what they said is true, he may need our help. The cargo decks are below us, so we are less likely to run into more of them."

"Are you sure it is safe?"

"Not entirely. But neither is staying here."

Kissa nodded. "Yes, you are probably right."

Neither of us moved.

"I can take the stairs to the observation deck and work my way down, if you want to start here and work your way up?"

Again, Kissa nodded.

"Alright, then." I rose and was halfway out the door when she reached out to take hold of my wrist.

"Be careful, Valentine," she said, then frowned.

"What is it?"

"Do you have a real name? Now that I know the story behind it, that one suits you even less than it did before."

"I did, once. But it never suited me, either."

"How does Val sound?"

I gazed down upon the decidedly voluptuous woman and felt myself respond to the quiet intensity in her eyes. Not for the first time, I wondered what she was doing here. What did she hope to gain? Why had she really come? There were so many questions I wanted to ask. Instead, I said the only thing I could say with a nobleman's life quite possibly hanging in the balance.

"Val works."

XI

PLOTS & SCHEMES

*T*he sea reflected the glare of the afternoon sun, glittering so far below the observation deck that to me it looked like a painting laid flat—deep blue hues with pockets of turquoise and teal splashed across a rippled canvas. I had never before seen the Mare Nostrum from such heights. Skyships occasionally hugged the coastline by necessity, but rarely ventured further—something to do with being unable to weather the storms that raged over such waters, if memory served.

I leaned over the railing, exhausted and perplexed. Though I had every intention of searching for the Archduke in due time, finding out how far off course we had flown had been my true objective for coming here. Now that I had my answer, however, I was more baffled than before.

Had we flown deep into the heart of Arabia or even north into Iberia, I might have understood. While both countries had close-knit ties to the Empire, neither would have passed on an opportunity to claim jurisdiction over a renegade skyship that had invaded their lands. In the hands of their engineers, the *Ex Machina*'s proprietary design could be very valuable. Indeed, that was the sole theory I had been able to come up with while trudging up the many flights of service stairs. Instead, here we were soaring west as though towards Rome itself. But why go through all this trouble if all they intended was to jump ship? Nothing was adding up.

I caught my reflection in the glass and was reminded of the physician's waxen complexion, his corpse surrounded by shuffling feet as passengers pushed and shoved each other. That boy and his mother. The man I stabbed to death beneath the strobe of a ventlamp. All that senseless chaos, all that needless death—and for what?

I started to step away from the railing and froze. Voices, garbled but unmistakable, sounded on the other side of the double doors. I hurriedly searched for a place to hide and happened to spy a series of concave nooks and crannies carved into the wall. I raced to the closest one and crouched, my back pressed against its curve, my stolen dagger drawn.

The doors creaked open.

"...the incident with the skyship's captain was unfortunate, I agree."

"Why was he not paid off like the others?"

"He was. Apparently, he got cold feet. As I understand it, he was under the impression Feretti would have his family killed if he were ever found out."

A chill ran up my spine as the voices became more and more distinct. The first might have belonged to the leader of the Mercantiles—the man who had ordered our capture and whom the others presumably referred to as Boss. The second, however, I was far more certain of.

"Oh, he would have," said the Archduke. "He still may, though it is possible the captain's actions will earn his family some leniency, now that he is dead. Feretti may even be gracious and send the family some coin. It is hard to tell with him. Is that all you have to report?"

"There were a few additional complications, but nothing outside our predictions, barring that mishap. There were several civilians injured in the aftermath, but we were able to subdue them all, eventually."

"Were any of your men hurt?"

"When the skyship banked? A few, but nothing major. We had already dealt with the staff, so they were the least affected. Bumps and bruises, mostly."

"No, I meant in general."

"Ah. There were a couple skirmishes, of course. One in the service corridor on a lower floor, it seems, got quite violent. Three of my men dead, and their killers were able to escape."

"Really? It is not like you to leave loose ends."

"No, it is not. But I was going to have to kill a few of them myself, otherwise, so it seemed like providence. Besides, we always knew there might be a few ruffians in the copper carts."

"And what of these killers? Could they have learned of our plan? The true reason you boarded this ship at my behest?"

"Not possible. I have not discussed your involvement with anyone—not even my second. My men care only that I pay them what they are owed. They know better than to ask questions they would rather not know the answers to."

"Glad to hear it."

"So," the Boss began after a moment's silence, "do you think all this will be enough to convince the Florentines to start hiring armed troops?"

"I do. My representative is already in talks with two of the Five to provide additional security. Feretti was bound to be the sole voice of dissension, but now, even if he disapproves, the Florentine will have no choice but to support the measure lest he look foolish in front of his peers. If that fails, we will blackmail him with what we found in the vaults. Either way, we get what we want."

"And the other part of your plan?"

"There was no helping it. Not with Adler's daughter and the Purifier on board. Which reminds me, you are certain neither were harmed?"

"They were better off than you were when we found you. I sent men down to check on them after you awoke, but the lower decks are too chaotic now that the rest are on the cargo deck preparing to jump."

"No matter, I am sure they are fine."

"And you? How fares the arm?"

"It hurts, but I cannot complain. If anything, it will only further my cause. With proof of my ordeal staring him in the face, the Praetor will have no choice but to toast my survival and my bravery. Besides, it looks far less suspicious this way. Even Feretti will not suspect I had a hand in this. Not once his men find me beaten and tied up."

"Ah, so you still want to go through with that?"

"One or two punches ought to do it. Try not to knock loose any of my teeth, or I will have trouble eating our dear Anna's cooking."

"She will be glad to see you. Now that the Archduchess is to be wed, she has few tasks to keep her occupied."

"Not to worry. I would not waste someone of her caliber. When I return, the three of us should discuss another scheme I have in mind. Discreetly, of course.

The voices began to fade as the two men retreated towards the door. I considered poking my head out but decided it would be far too great a risk. Given everything I had just heard, I would be lucky to leave this room alive.

"And what scheme is that?" the leader asked.

"Though I am loath to say it, I think my mother may have outlived her usefulness. Perhaps if she were to fall ill, a nurse could slip—"

The doors swung shut.

A.D. X KAL. APR. MMCDLIII A.U.C.

APRIL 3RD, 1770

Carcer on the Outskirts of Cappadocia

Contra felicem vix deus vires habet.

Against a lucky man a god scarcely has power.

SKYSHIPS

OVER CONSTANTINOPLE

I

INTERLUDE: CAESAR'S TOMB

*F*rom above, the seemingly endless canopy of Constantinople's red clay rooftops is broken up by a handful of towering, man-made structures: the Byzantium cathedral built by Justinian I with its four jutting spires; the triple-tiered, nigh impregnable walls that encircle the entire peninsula; the Hippodrome with its meticulously combed racetrack, its bizarre litter of mismatched statues, and its monolithic obelisks; and, of course, the Imperial Palace to which all others pay homage in one way or another—itself a rather drab, white quartz stronghold spruced up by gardens so lush and vibrant that not even the cerulean waters of the Golden Horn could compete.

And yet, not one of these feats of engineering holds so much as a contra-band candle to that architectural marvel which can be seen the instant one dips below the clouds. For looming on the peninsula opposite the sprawling metropolis like some lofty sentinel, the pyramid known as Caesar's Tomb towers over every other structure in sight, its precious metal topper blazing in the noonday sun like the light of a distant star.

The monument, designed to dwarf those found in the necropolis outside Cairo in both proportion and pageantry, was a testament to the superiority of New Rome. Having seen the crumbling remains of Giza for myself some years back, it was hard to deny their success. From its gleaming coat of alabaster paint to the polished gold cap that formed its pinnacle, the Tomb embodied the heart and soul of New Rome—a city so gargantuan that it straddled two peninsulas and so grandiose that it had outshone every other for centuries.

Or so they would have you believe.

II

A GLASS OF BRANDY & HOLD THE LIES

I watched Constantinople grow larger from a bar that doubled as a modest observatory—a middle deck establishment that allowed passengers to pay for the privilege of peering out at the horizon through plate-sized portholes while getting bleary-eyed drunk. No one had been charged on this particular morning, of course; in hopes of improving morale and salvaging their vessel's tarnished reputation, the crew had agreed to ease the usual restrictions.

It was not working.

"I heard they jumped off before Signore Feretti's men came aboard," a shabbily dressed woman said to her companion two tables over, their gazes locked on a soldier in checkered livery standing against the far wall. "Useless, the lot of them. Where were they when our rooms were being tossed and our things riffled through?"

"Did they really jump? Into the sea?"

"They say a ship was waiting for them, and that they used our bedsheets to slow their fall. But do you know what else they took? Nothing! Or at least nothing the crew will talk about. Quite the mystery."

The two women's voices fell to hushed whispers as Feretti's hireling straightened and walked among the tables, one hand resting upon the pommel of his rapier, pausing only to peer out the nearby porthole.

"I do not trust them," the woman's companion said once the Florentine was well out of earshot.

"That is because you are not a fool, dear."

The companion made a pleased sound in the back of her throat before continuing. "You know, the steward I spoke to said several people died. I wonder if they'll be giving out compensation?"

"Oh, I don't doubt it, especially..."

Tired of eavesdropping, I held up my empty glass and signaled to the nearest waiter. He rushed to fulfill my request, weaving between tables filled with hollow-eyed survivors and rumour-mongers alike. Unsurprisingly, it was the affluent in their vibrant finery who appeared the most frazzled—like brightly-coloured birds whose cages had been rattled.

As if the thought alone had conjured him, the orchestrator of all our woes ducked through the velvet partition at the far end of the hall. The Archduke was dressed all in black but for a high, stiff-necked collar and an Imperial red *pileus* set like an overturned bowl atop his head—a vulture having come to peck out our eyes.

"Herr Valentine, there you are!" he cried, drawing scowls from the other patrons.

It took every gram of restraint I had not to stand up and walk out as the foul bastard settled into the chair opposite me. Unfortunately, there was little else I could do; knowing what he had done was not the same as being able to prove it. Besides, I had no jurisdiction here. The Archduke may have been a monster, but he was not the sort I was allowed to put down.

A pity, I know.

"Here I am," I replied, hiding my revulsion behind a beleaguered smile.

"It took me nearly an hour to track you down, I will have you know," the Archduke said, sounding bemused rather than exasperated. "They insisted I was to see a doctor first thing this morning, or I would have done so, sooner. Are you well?"

"As well as can be expected."

The Archduke nodded. "I had thought to invite Fraulein Adler and yourself to dine with me and perhaps enjoy the meal we were denied yesterday, but I can see now you have found an equally agreeable form of sustenance."

The Archduke eyed the glass of brandy the waiter set before me and signaled for the same with his good hand. The other was hidden within the sling that cradled his broken arm. His face, I was pleased to note, had been similarly mistreated. Indeed, the scar on his brow looked dainty compared to the puffy skin of his mouth and the split lip he kept inadvertently probing with his tongue. I could hardly sympathise, of course, though I could relate; my own flesh was littered with all manner of scrapes and bruises.

"Quite the establishment you have found here," the Archduke continued. "I had never thought to find a drink on the middle decks. Tell me, do they keep it this dim on purpose? Does it add some sort of ambience?"

I shrugged and took a sip of my drink, not entirely trusting myself to speak. Nero was right: I simply could not tolerate a liar. In fact, I found it hard not to fantasise about stringing up the smug piece of shit from that sling he wore, or maybe chucking him off the cargo deck without a bedsheet.

"Herr Valentine?" The Archduke waved a hand in front of my face. "Did you hear what I said?"

"No, sorry."

"I merely hoped to apologise for not being there with you and Fraulein Adler. She told me what you both went through to escape. How harrowing that must have been! Of course, there was nothing I could do given my unconscious state, but I assure you I would have much preferred fighting at your side than being held hostage by those vile Mercantiles."

"I wouldn't be so sure of that, Archduke," I replied, swirling my drink so I would not have to meet his eye. "I cannot imagine a man like you enjoys getting his hands dirty."

It was not a particularly subtle jab, but it did not matter; the nobleman was not listening. Instead, his attention had shifted to the striking woman who approached our table. With so many of her tattoos covered beneath a high-necked, long sleeved gown and her wavy auburn locks piled high upon her head in artful ringlets, it took me a few seconds longer to recognise Kissa than it might have, otherwise.

The Amazon and I had yet to speak again since parting ways the previous day, though I had caught sight of her in passing before the Florentines all but locked us in our respective cabins for the night while they sorted out the mess the would-be Mercantiles had left behind. Still, I was not as pleased to see her as I might have been a few minutes prior; the fact that she had found time to regale the Archduke with tales of our exploits had left an understandably bad taste in my mouth.

The Archduke rose and cleared his throat as Kissa arrived. "Fraulein, forgive me. I did not know you would be joining us. Allow me to order you a drink? Perhaps a glass of bubbling white. It may be too early in the day for red."

"It is too early in the day for a great many things, Your Grace," Kissa replied as she took the seat between us. "But I would not say no to a glass of Visigothian, if they carry it."

The Archduke arched an eyebrow but passed on the woman's order when the waiter arrived. He cleared his throat as if to speak, though he waited until the attention Kissa's entrance had brought to die down before doing so.

"To what do we owe the pleasure of such a modest outfit, Fraulein?"

"Feretti's men," Kissa replied, rolling her eyes. "They insisted I would be confined to my cabin if I tried to walk about with my arms and legs on display. The stewards likely put them up to it."

"I must admit I am surprised you let them intimidate you. The girl I knew would have broken their fingers for trying. Indeed, I seem to recall you making a habit of such things."

"That only happened once, Your Grace, and your cousin deserved it. Besides, they do not intimidate me. Resistance would simply have proven more hassle than it was worth."

"Well, I for one think you look splendid. Would you not agree, Herr Valentine?"

"I..." I trailed off, shaking my head. "I apologise, but would you both excuse me?"

The Archduke cocked his head, quizzically. "Is something wrong?"

"No, nothing," I lied. "I find myself ill-suited to conversation at the moment, that's all."

The truth, of course, was that after everything the Archduke had done—after seeing firsthand how little those deaths his draconian plans had caused weighed on him—I simply could not stomach listening to his inane banter for a minute longer. Worse still, I could not yet be sure whether Kissa had been involved—a suspicion which turned their every word and deed into a coded, callous exchange.

"Are you unwell?" Kissa asked. "Were you hurt?"

I waved that away. "No, nothing like that, Fraulein Adler."

The Amazon frowned and placed her hand over mine. "Then are you sure you cannot be convinced to stay? You do owe me a drink for saving your life, after all. And we should begin discussing what to do once we have docked."

"Another time." I struggled not to look at the Archduke as I drew my hand away and scooted my chair back. "You and I can decide our next move once we reach Constantinople. If I don't see you before then, meet me at the base of the tower."

"Have I missed something?" the Archduke interjected as I prepared to rise, his eyes dancing back and forth between the Amazon and me.

Kissa frowned. "Your Grace?"

"I believe Herr Valentine would prefer to speak with you in private, Fraulein. If so, please, allow me to take my leave, instead. I do not wish to meddle in matters of the heart." The Archduke grinned at the two of us, his eyes twinkling with amusement. "Unless of course you two are keeping a secret from me. Something to do with my excavation site, perhaps?"

"Do not be silly," Kissa replied, though the faintest blush did indeed rise in her cheeks. "If anything, Herr Valentine is feeling guilty."

"Whatever for?"

"For never having found you once we escaped."

"You went searching for me?" The Archduke pressed a hand to his chest. "Herr Valentine, I am touched."

"We both did, actually," I replied, hoping to steer the conversation into safer waters.

"Both of you? My, how blessed I am to have such caring companions!"

"Exactly my point," Kissa added. "Herr Valentine searched every floor from the observation deck to the dining room. He has nothing to be ashamed of."

"All the way to the observation deck, you say?" The Archduke's smug smile wilted at the edges. "And when was this?"

"I never made it," I lied, staring at the floor so as to hide my troubled expression. "Fraulein Adler was right. I am embarrassed, just not for the reason she thinks. The truth is I got winded and had to rest long before I reached the upper decks."

"Think nothing of it," the Archduke replied magnanimously, though I could see suspicion lurking behind his eyes. "It was a trying time for us all.

"I appreciate that, Your Grace. Still, I should get back to my cabin and write Nero before we disembark." I finished my drink and reached for the purse of coins I kept in the lining of my jacket. "He will want to know what happened, especially since it will mean a further delay."

"Of course. But please, put your purse away."

"Your Grace?"

"You may not know this, Herr Valentine, but my family honours many arcane traditions. One of which is that all men must part ways with neither owing the other. This way, should those men never meet again, they do so as equals. Given what you have done for me, not to mention the many, many uncertainties the future holds, you must allow me to settle our account."

"Very well. If you insist, Your Grace."

"I do. Please, do take care, Herr Valentine." The Archduke raised his glass in a mocking salute. "Take very great care."

III

INTERLUDE: CONSTANTINOPLE

*I*n Constantinople, there is no such thing as a quiet street. From sunrise to sunset, even its widest thoroughfares become a congested bustle of man and machine as whistlecoaches shaped like canal boats—the pitch of their shrieks an octave higher than those of the boxier iterations to the west—weave between pedestrians while six generations of skyships drift overhead, casting shadows like storm clouds as they pass.

In the heart of the city sit the market districts where miniature bazaars erected by enterprising vendors crowd coveted street corners and clog up alleyways, catering to foreigners and natives alike in a clash of skin colors, fashions, and tongues. Indeed, it is said that in Constantinople you can buy anything your heart desires, so long as you are willing to pay a great deal more for it than what it is worth.

To the south, along the tip of the larger peninsula, there is the Palace Grounds—sprawling villas owned by young plutocrats and old money. To the east, the trade guilds surrounding Highbridge and its Gold Coast, occupied by those too wealthy to be ignored, but not yet influential enough to be remembered. And then, beneath the shadow of Caesar's Tomb and across the bay, Lowbridge and the Bronze Coast with its crafter's guilds and trade workers.

To the west and opposite both is the Waterfront, a rowdy entertainment district perpetually cluttered with whatever the sea happens to drag in:

traders, merchants, sailors, soldiers, pirates, and slaves. Unlike the others, the Waterfront discourages residential occupation, though it does boast the very worst bars and very best brothels.

To the north sit the ghettos that plague every city no matter how grandiose: Wallings and Gateside. The former is a repository for all things disreputable, while the latter is nothing but a sad, impoverished sanctuary for those who have nowhere else to go.

Of course, such squalor may be found no matter which way one turns. Whether it be the trash piled up against the sides of buildings like lawn clippings, its foul odor mingled with the funk of unwashed bodies and the intolerable reek of piss; the copper-tinged snot left behind on stone walls and paved streets by the spice bark addicts; or the freshly knifed corpses which have to be fetched from the harbour every morning by a crew paid for by the Praetor, himself. I can assure you something unpleasant awaits around every corner of that sprawling city.

And do not even get me started on the monsters.

IV

FEEDERS

"*I*s something wrong, Signore?"

The porter who spoke, an elderly Moor in a double-breasted jacket that seemed particularly ill-suited to the morning's heat, trailed after me with my rucksack loaded on his rickety cart. Those who had traveled without luggage had been allowed to disembark first and could be seen mingling amongst the crowds up ahead, many of them bandaged or limping.

"No, nothing. Just getting my bearings." I lowered my head and continued walking, doing my best to ignore the near constant barrage of jostling and the glares that came with it.

Constantinople's skyport was a chaotic jumble of people heading to and fro—some halting in their tracks to check departure and arrival times, others rushing headlong into the fray with their own porters in tow, and then of course there were those already queued up on the easternmost terrace, clustered outside the skylifts like herded sheep.

From its remarkable heights, I could see all of Highbridge spread out before me, its many lending houses overshadowed by the sloping architectural landmark for which the borough had been named. To my left, sunlight flared across the waters of the Golden Horn, its placid surface a crisp shade of blue along the edges and amber in the middle. A brisk wind whipped at my hair and flipped my collar as I leaned out to peer down at the city directly below.

The porter coughed politely. "This is as far as I go, Signore."

"Right, sorry. Here, hand that over."

With difficulty, the porter hefted my rucksack, holding it just long enough for me to slip my arms through the sturdy leather straps. I grunted as he let go, aware of the weight in a way I had not been even a few months ago.

"Will that be all, Signore?"

"One moment." I was patting down my person, hunting for a loose coin I could throw his way, when I noticed a slew of yellow-green tents surrounding the skyport. I froze, my gut churning at the sight. "What are they doing here?"

The porter peered down and rubbed at his balding scalp. "You mean the trappers? They are down there most days, Signore."

Though technically accurate, I shook my head in disgust at the benign appellation. I preferred to call the bastards what they were: feeders. Of course, those who dealt in the creatures we Purifiers hunt had a variety of names. Trappers, carvers, feeders, black-couriers, and devil-runners—these were but a few of the titles bestowed upon those opportunistic procurers of the macabre and the exotic.

"Call them whatever you like," I said. "It doesn't change what they are, or what they do. Nor does it change the law. They should not be on this side of the bridge. Their wares are dangerous."

The porter squinted up at me as though he could not decide if I was joking, his mouth caught somewhere between a smile and a sneer. "This is Constantinople, Signore. If a man has something to sell, he must sell it. That is the only law that anyone cares about here."

I grunted, wondering whether the porter knew just what he was condoning; while their industry may have fueled commerce and furthered alchemical innovation—thereby earning them the tacit support of many governments—it did not change the fact that the feeders made their living by exploiting that which we sought to eradicate. Indeed, had the porter seen for himself the dismembered limbs twitching for hours on end or the jellied orbs floating in glowing jars, their viridescent pupils tracking one's every move, I had to believe he would have sung a far different tune.

By the time I thought to say as much, however, the old man had already shuffled off. Perhaps he had grown tired of waiting for his tip, or perhaps he felt I was simply not worth the trouble. Lifelong residents of cities such as these often reacted to me that way—as if disdaining urbanity and all its loathsome trappings meant I was an unworthy, uncultured fool.

With a resigned sigh, I adjusted my rucksack and hoofed it to the nearest skylift, waiting for several minutes before piling in with thirty or so others. From there, it was not long before I reached the square where Kissa and I had arranged to meet.

Once there, I scanned the crowd but saw no trace of the Amazon. Thinking to distract myself while I waited, I wandered over to the nearest stall. There, a vendor held up a birdcage at eye level. Within the cage hung a dozen or so disturbingly humanoid creatures no bigger than my thumb, each of which looked as though they had been smothered in wax and dipped in green glass. Their wispy arms had been pulled taut above their heads, their wrists bound by dainty silver chains not unlike those a harem dancer might wear about her ankles.

Disturbed by the sight of those impossibly rare, exceptionally prohibited creatures, I wandered over to listen to the merchant as he rocked his cage from side to side, luring an audience the way one might bait a cat. When he spoke, his voice was almost conspiratorial—as though confessing his sins to the gathered crowd.

Which, in some ways, I suppose he was.

"These devious creatures you see before you, my fellow citizens, are known as Burrowers," he declared. "It is said the Armenians trained them to delve inside men's ears and feast on their brains, driving their victims mad and leaving behind nothing but corpses with empty skulls. Found throughout the deserts of Arabia, they are known to rise up from the sands in the hundreds, like a swarm of flesh-eating insects."

His audience drew back at his description, both revolted and dismayed.

"Yes, I know! A truly horrible fate, and one that should be avoided at all costs."

"But how?" a member of the crowd asked.

"I am glad you asked, my friend!" The vendor snatched up a jar filled with a lumpy brown substance from a nearby table. "The answer is beeswax! But not just any beeswax. My jars include a special tincture tested upon these very creatures. See how it has tamed them? Buy my product, and never again will you or your loved ones fear the sound of their gnawing teeth as they gorge on your brain. And that does not even include its many other, equally advantageous uses!"

"What are they?"

"Another excellent question! Allow me to list them all, beginning with its many cosmetic benefits..."

I drifted away, shaking my head at the vendor's self-serving lies. The creatures he held captive were neither Burrowers nor Arabian. In fact, the Picks—or Picksies, as they were sometimes called—were diminutive beings that took particular issue with anything locked, be it doors, chests, or even vaults. Native to my own country, the Picks could only be captured during the day, at which point they became so lethargic one could easily trap them beneath an overturned bowl.

The moment the sun fell below the horizon, however, those once docile creatures were bound to rage inside their metal prison, jerking against their shackles like silent string puppets, for they have no voices. No eyes, ears, mouths, or noses. Just smooth, formless faces. And yet, when they writhed, it was as though you could *feel* their screams.

"You look troubled."

I turned, startled to find Kissa standing not a few paces away. "I'm sorry, Fraulein. Did I leave you waiting long?"

"Not terribly long, no." Kissa eyed the stalls at my back. "Were you hoping to do some shopping before we set out?"

"No, I simply wanted a better look at what that man over there was selling."

Kissa followed my gaze to the yellow-green canopy beneath which the enterprising vendor had already begun selling jars of beeswax to thick-skulled foreigners. The Amazon wrinkled her nose in distaste.

"What a revolting way to earn a living," she said.

I nodded.

"Anyway," she continued, "we should get going."

"Where to?"

"I thought we might start by paying a visit to an old acquaintance of my father's who might be willing to trade information. Unless you have a better idea."

"No, that sounds like as good a place to begin as any. Where does this friend of your father live?"

"Acquaintance," Kissa corrected. "I honestly have no idea where Mustafa lives. Probably somewhere far nicer than one might expect. But his shop is in Wallings, which is where we must go to speak to him."

I frowned. "What sort of business is he in?"

"He collects things. Artifacts. Scrolls. Maps. And, most importantly, information." Kissa nudged me. "Why, does his place of business bother you?"

"Of course not," I lied.

"Well, it should. Wallings is every bit as bad as its reputation suggests, and even it is too good for Mustafa. My father loathes the man, mostly because he so often turns out to be right, but also because he keeps proposing to me in front of his wives."

I looked over to find Kissa smirking.

"You're teasing me."

"I am. It seemed you could use the distraction. It is something about this place, yes? It clearly bothers you."

"It does."

"Then let us leave it behind." Kissa looped her arm through mine and drew me away. The Amazon had ditched her dress in favor of a bib front shirt tucked into a pair of pantaloons swallowed at the knees by a pair of black leather boots. The hairstyle she had kept, though I assumed that was only because it would have been a bigger fuss to change it.

As we left, I cast a lingering look over my shoulder at the other stalls. In doing so, I noticed a bevy of fresh horrors, not least of which included a witch-wood box and the pale, hairless arm of a ghoul it contained. The dismembered limb clawed at its cage like a dog after a bone not ten feet from a gaggle of wide-eyed children with terrified expressions slapped across their doughy faces.

"Perhaps we should discuss something else," Kissa suggested. "Something that will put your mind at ease."

"What did you have in mind?"

"I have to come up with the suggestion as well as the solution? That hardly seems fair."

"Why not tell me more about your relationship with the Archduke?" I blurted out the question before I could stop myself, provoked perhaps by the nagging suspicion that they were closer than their snarky banter suggested.

"I cannot see how that is any of your concern," Kissa replied, haltingly. "But it is easily accomplished. Joseph and I have no relationship."

"And yet you call him by his first name."

"I refuse to call him anything else unless I must." Kissa let out a beleaguered sigh. "The situation is...complicated. Our families were once quite close. My father's family and Joseph's, that is. In fact, my father and his father were childhood friends. All but inseparable, to hear my grandmother tell it."

"What happened?"

"It is a long story."

"It's a long walk."

Kissa released my arm to make way for a group of rowdy youths as they came racing down the street, howling and jeering. I listened for the cry of a city guard stopping them, but there was none. Odd, I thought, considering there were two of them trailing not far behind us.

"I was born and raised among my mother's people until I was thirteen," Kissa said, when at last she was able to rejoin me. "I knew very little about my father, then, though I saw him often. My mother was fond of him, I think, but he was still a man."

"Lesser."

"Exactly. But then my mother died, and I was sent to live with my grandmother in Vienna."

"You weren't taken in by someone else in your tribe? One of your relatives?"

"No. I was not welcome, not after what happened. And no, I do not wish to talk about it."

"I understand," I replied, sensing right away there was nothing to be gained by prying. "In any case, I am truly sorry for your loss."

"I appreciate that, but there is no need. It was a long time ago."

I rejected that notion immediately; no matter how many years had gone by, I could still remember the smell of my mother's hair. I could remember the shanties she used to sing as she hung our clothes to dry, or how she used to pinch my cheeks whenever I was frustrated or sad. Those memories, coupled with the sight of her lifeless corpse lying curled up like a little girl, were not the sort that faded.

"I don't think the wound of a mother's passing is something time, or anything else for that matter, can mend. It's like trying to draw breath with a stone block on your chest. Just because you can doesn't make it ache any less."

"I suppose you are right," Kissa replied, softening. "It does feel that way, sometimes."

"Was Vienna to your liking?" I asked a few minutes later, cringing inwardly at my clumsy attempt to change the subject.

"No, it was not. In fact, I loathed it there. I was a novelty from the moment I arrived; paraded before all the royal houses the way the Nubians show off their giant cats. They called me exotic, a term I learned to despise almost as much as the word rare, if you can believe it."

I chuckled at that.

Kissa smirked. "When I came of age, my grandmother and I paid the Habsburgs a great many visits. I think she hoped I would befriend one of Joseph's younger sisters, or that I might catch the eye of the Archduke, himself. But then Joseph's father passed, and my father fell out of favour. At the time, I understood very little of it all. As far as I was concerned, one day I was allowed to visit the Habsburg estate whenever I wished, and the next I was not."

"And you've had no contact with them since?"

"None. I left Vienna after my grandmother passed to join my father on his expeditions. In fact, I have not even spared a thought for Joseph in years —nor him for me, I expect. I doubt he would have remembered me at all had I not asked to accompany you."

"You wanted to come?"

Kissa arched an eyebrow. "Of course. Is that so surprising?"

"Now that I know you? Not in the least. But your father did lead us to believe you were being sent because he did not trust us."

"Of course he did. First of all, no one sends me anywhere. And secondly, it is not you he does not trust, though I do not doubt he implied as much."

"If not us, then..." I clapped a hand to my head. "The Archduke. That's why you kept asking after him."

"And accepting his invitations," Kissa added, nodding. "My father does not trust he will keep his word and stay silent about the site. Not now that he has seen the helmet. Fortunately, being held hostage and having his arm broken may have put a damper on his plans, at least for the time being."

"I would not count on it."

"You may be right. Still, I doubt he will make a move until he has found a way to lift the curse. And for that, he still needs us."

"I hope you are right."

For both our sakes, I added, silently.

V

RUMOURS

Our destination was a leaning warehouse with shuttered windows above which jutted tattered awnings that might have been red once but had since faded to a mottled shade of pink. A furled flag hung limp beside a crooked door, and the stoop was covered in a layer of dirt and sand. But then, that was what one should expect from Wallings; caught between the modest walls of Constantine's era and those three-tiered behemoths erected by his successor, this neighbourhood was a haven for tenants and transients, alike.

Kissa paused with her hand on the door. "No matter what Mustafa says to you, do not take it personally. He loves getting a reaction out of someone and is far better at it than most. Trust me. In fact, you would be better off playing dumb."

I nodded in understanding.

"Excellent. Just like that."

"Funny."

"I thought so."

Inside the shop, pots of various shapes and sizes filled the entire room, some stacked so high they formed precarious columns that brushed the ceiling, others so large they doubled as walls. Kissa gestured for me to follow and wove between rows of assorted crockery with the expertise of one who has done so many times. After several turns, we reached an unobstructed patch of tile floor caked liberally in sand—like some forlorn beach upon which so many tubs of clay and metal urns had washed ashore.

On the far side of that space, a squat, obese man sat hunched over a cluttered desk, cursing first in Greek, then Arabic, and finally what sounded suspiciously like the sing-songy language of the Caesarean islanders. He hastily scribbled on a piece of parchment, his great big, greasy black beard quivering like a disturbed bush.

"Ahem," Kissa coughed.

The pot merchant did not look up. "Come back later, I am busy."

"Are you sure?" Kissa asked. "I came all this way, after all."

Mustafa jerked his head up and leapt to his feet, holding out both arms like a priest bestowing a blessing. "Kissa, my love! You have returned to me, at last. Come, let us embrace like the lovers we were always fated to become!"

"I would rather not."

"Ah, yes, you are right. The day is far too young to see our passion ignite, though I dare say the sun itself would become jealous of our heat. But who is this you bring with you? Wait, let me guess! He is a gift! An early wedding present, yes? I must tell you he is a bit on the scrawny side for a manservant, but then as they say: it is the thought that matters. I thank you from the bottom of my heart."

"Herr Mustafa, allow me to introduce Herr Valentine," Kissa replied in her blandest tone, all but ignoring the merchant's inane chatter. "He is a Purifier."

"Ah, one of Octavian's dogs!" Mustafa thrust a finger in the air. "Tell me, Signore Valentine, do you require special compensation for putting down ordinary vermin? I have this rodent problem, you see—"

An ominous crash sounded in the other room followed immediately by furtive whispers, the scuff of footsteps, and the creak of rusty hinges.

"Ah, there goes one, now," Mustafa drawled, massaging the bridge of his nose. "Rat! Get in here!"

A boy of perhaps twelve or thirteen poked his head out from a nearby doorway just as, somewhere behind him, a door bounced off a wall. The child wore a cap and scarf that hid all but his freckled cheeks and dark, thickly-lashed eyes. He flicked those at each of us in turn, then squinted.

"T'wasn't me who broke it," the boy insisted, his voice muffled beneath the scarf. "It was Faruq. He wished to see if he could fit in that new urn you bought. The one with the bone inlay. He was very insistent."

"The new…" Mustafa groaned. "And am I supposed to believe Faruq, little Faruq who can barely remember to put on pants before leaving his mother's house, came up with this idea all on his own?"

"…yes?"

"Then tell him to come out. I will hear what happened from his own mouth."

"Oh, he left."

"Because you told him you would stay behind and take the blame, I think." Mustafa raked his fingers through his sheeny beard until they came away glistening with oil. "What am I to do with you, boy?"

"You could teach me that trick with the knife you showed Faruq last week? He would not shut up about how you used it to gut that man from—"

"That," Mustafa hissed, "was not a story he was meant to share. Bah! Come then. Since you are here, come and make yourself useful."

The boy shrugged and slipped into the room, grabbing a vase by the handle as he came. He tossed it in the air, let it spin end over end, and caught it mere inches from the floor in one smooth, practiced motion. Mustafa gasped, waddled over, and snatched the vase out of the boy's hands with a proprietary air.

"What do you think you are doing?!"

"You said to make myself useful."

"And how was that useful?"

"I thought I would juggle for your guests. I saw an Armenian do it last week with six knives. Should I use more pots?"

"More…" Mustafa tugged on the child's scarf, revealing a grin as wide as any I had ever seen. He swatted at the boy, who danced out of reach with a laugh.

"Is that a no?"

"You must think you are very clever," Mustafa said, scowling. "Perhaps I ought to hang you from the rafters by your toes and beat that out of you."

"You would have to catch me, first, Uncle."

Mustafa grunted and made a shooing motion with both hands. "You are not worth the trouble. Now run and fetch us a bottle of the blue. And be quick about it."

"Of course, Uncle." The boy meandered through another doorway all but hidden behind a mound of shattered pottery. Within seconds, I could hear him rummaging around as cabinets slammed closed and bottles clinked.

"And you best not even think of stealing anything, or I will pay a visit to my sister! We shall see how funny you think you are, then."

"Yes, Uncle!"

"Someone far less tolerant than I is going to cut out that tongue of his, one day," Mustafa muttered before turning to us and clapping his hands together. "Now, Kissa, my heart, where were we? Oh yes! You were saying you have finally come to your senses and agreed to make me the luckiest man alive by becoming my betrothed. Please, let us continue where we left off. I believe we were discussing my raw sexual appeal and your insatiable Amazonian appetites."

"Last I heard you already had a wife, Mustafa. Two of them."

"Three, actually," the merchant replied, unabashedly. "My youngest brother died, leaving poor Faruq without a father and his young widow without a husband. Very regrettable. Naturally, I had to step in and provide them with the love and care they both deserve."

"Naturally," Kissa echoed, drily.

"What can I say, I am an honourable man." Mustafa made a show of bowing before swinging his beady little gaze to me. "Is this manservant you brought me a mute? One does hear things about the trauma his Order inflicts upon its initiates. That arena business, very cruel."

"I speak," I replied. "But only when I have something worthwhile to say. Unlike some."

"Ah, well said! There may be hope for you yet, manservant."

The boy came wobbling back into the room with a glass bottle painted blue and covered in dust, his face flushed and breath reeking of alcohol. The merchant took both the bottle and the boy by the neck and shook them.

"What did I say about getting into the wine? And what are we to do with this? Glasses, you fool boy! Bring us cups."

"They were all dirty," the child wheezed. "You told Faruq to clean them, remember? I really think you should have a talk with him. He has been very disrespectful, lately."

"Caesar, give me the strength..." Mustafa mumbled. The merchant released the boy and downed a third of the bottle's contents right in front of us, smacking his lips as he lowered it. "That is better. Well, it seems traditional hospitality is out of the question, so I shall dispense with the formalities altogether. Why have you come to see me, Kissa?"

"We need information," Kissa replied. She held out a hand for the bottle and was quickly rewarded. "Nothing sensitive. Historical only."

"And yet what you propose promises to be an expensive conversation, all the same. Are you sure you wish to ask me and not one of your father's so-called experts? History is their specialty, is it not?"

"Scholars do not put as much faith in rumours as you do. Also, we are dealing with something my father's contacts might have a proprietary interest in. For your silence in that regard, I will gladly pay the usual fee. For the information itself, however, I was hoping we could make a deal. A trade."

Mustafa grunted. "And what is it you believe you know that I do not?"

"Do you have any disciplinary tips?" the boy chimed in, helpfully. "Because Uncle could really use those."

"That is enough out of you!" Mustafa lunged for the lad, who scampered off into the other room with a high pitched squeal that gave way to giggles.

"Well, that depends," Kissa replied, fighting not to laugh herself. "How much do you know about the skyship that was commandeered a couple days ago?"

Mustafa shrugged. "Only what my eyes and ears at the Highbridge skyport have told me. They say Mercantiles killed the captain and took the staff and passengers hostage. It is newsworthy, of course, but anything on so grand a scale is of little value to me. My customers come to me for well-guarded secrets whispered behind locked doors, not what they could find out for themselves by craning their ears on the street."

"And if I told you that it was not Mercantiles who took the ship?"

"Interesting." Mustafa patted at his beard, shaping it with his hands while sizing up the two of us. "A question for a question?"

Kissa groaned. "Must we? I was hoping we might exchange information like two consenting adults."

"Was that your first question?"

"Was that yours?"

"Very good!" Mustafa clapped his meaty palms together for the second time. "I have always enjoyed this game, but it is only with you that I feel so stimulated. You may begin."

"Gracious of you." Kissa took a swig from the bottle while she considered what to say, though her voice came out hoarse when next she spoke. "What do you know of those who first called Cappadocia home? Not the Greeks. This would have been centuries before their time."

"What an intriguing question! I must assume your father has found himself another promising archaeological puzzle. The answer is, I am afraid, less so. No records of that period have survived, so anything I tell you would be pure speculation…"

Kissa gestured for him to continue.

"Very well. In the centuries before Rome was founded, many ancient kings and queens were rumoured to have come to Anatolia. Some to conquer, others to pay their respects. It is said that the terra-cotta priests who live in the shadows of Cappadocia's mountains are remnants of those who once invaded the region, or at the very least disciples of the old religions. Perhaps your father has found something of theirs from that long ago time?"

Kissa frowned, then nodded. "Your turn."

"Excellent. If not the Mercantiles, who took control of the skyship? And, in the spirit of openness, how did you come by this knowledge? If it turns out you are peddling someone else's half-truths, I shall be very disappointed."

"The answer to that is simple, my friend. We were there. Though I cannot tell you who they were, not for certain. The men all wore senior steward clothing and spoke crudely, but without foreign accents. Likely Imperial auxiliaries, if I had to venture a guess. They took orders from a single man but acted more like mercenaries."

"Hmm…how curious. You are implying anyone might have been responsible, provided they had the means? I can think of a few who would pay a great deal to hear this, and at least one who would pay a great deal more to have it never be spoken of, again."

"I would be wary, if I were you, about whom I approach with that information," I cautioned.

"And why is that, my dear manservant?"

"You do not have to answer that," Kissa interjected. "It is not his turn."

I waved that off. "Think about it. If they, whoever they are, were willing to make an enemy of the Feretti family, do you really think they would risk leaving you alive? Would they risk leaving any of us alive?"

Kissa shot me an odd look, but Mustafa was already nodding.

"This is a wise thing you have said. Perhaps I will sell the lesser details. The senior steward uniforms, that will fetch a small amount. And weapons. What weapons did they use? And how did they escape? This is a mystery even to me."

"First," I said, "do you know anyone who might be able to tell us more about the history surrounding Cappadocia?"

"That depends. Perhaps if I knew more about what it is you seek…"

"Mustafa," Kissa warned.

"What? I do not inquire for myself, but for your sake and the sake of the children we shall one day raise together. I wish only to be of service to you and your noble father so that he might give you to me with a proper dowry, as is your people's custom."

"Very funny."

Mustafa made a show of bowing low before the Amazon. "If hoarding your secrets matters more to you than the truth, then I am afraid I can do—"

"There's a curse involved," I interjected, forestalling Kissa's objection with an upright hand. "We believe it may have something to do with the ruins Herr Doktor Adler has discovered. If we can determine which civilization the ruins belong to, we may be able to use their ancient rituals to lift it."

"A curse? How terrible!" Mustafa took a few furtive steps back and eyed us both up and down. "You are both…clean, yes?"

"We are. But it is threatening the lives of men who work for Fraulein Adler's father. They may very well be dead by now, but the longer we delay, the more likely that becomes. If you help us, the Order would be very grateful."

Mustafa rolled his eyes. "Your Order is already grateful. Octavian still owes me a cask of wine."

"Mustafa—" Kissa began.

"No, there is no need for that. I am not an unsympathetic man. You and your father are like family to me, despite our differences." Mustafa strolled over to his desk and plopped down in his chair. "There is one who may be able to answer your questions. The Signora of the Cisterns, she is called. It is said she is the last of a sect of priestesses who have passed down a complete verbal history spanning dozens of generations. If anyone could answer your question, I believe it would be her."

"How do we find her?" I asked.

"Ah, that is the easy part! The Signora is kept under constant guard below the Basilica. This is one of the city's poorest kept secrets and so of little cost to me. The difficulty lies in getting past those guards. As far as I am aware, an audience with the Signora can only be granted by Praetor Otho himself. So, unless someone very powerful happens to owe you a favour, I think you may be luckless."

Kissa and I exchanged glances.

"As a matter of fact..."

VI

WHEN OPPORTUNITY KNOCKS

A glimpse of the noonday sun confirmed we had spent at least an hour in Mustafa's shop. Though Kissa seemed satisfied by the exchange, I was hard pressed to say whether or not it was time well spent; while we had eventually supplied him with the pertinent details surrounding our ordeal on the *Ex Machina*, he had offered us nothing but conjecture and hypotheticals. Even his tip about this Signora of the Cisterns came with its fair share of uncertainties.

"I think we should reach out to Joseph," Kissa said, shielding her eyes from the sudden glare. "He will surely have the Praetor's ear. If he were to make the request today, we might be able to speak with this priestess before sundown."

"I don't think involving the Archduke is a good idea," I admitted.

"Why not?"

"Well, for one thing, I don't believe he has the clout. From what he told Nero and me, his relationship with the Praetor seems tenuous, at best. Asking for a favour the very day he arrives might be asking too much."

Kissa scowled. "Even if that is true, I still think we should ask. Perhaps Joseph will see that it is worth the risk to his reputation."

I was still contemplating my reply when Kissa grabbed me by both arms and stepped in close, staring up into my face as though moments from pressing her lips to mine.

"Is it my imagination," she whispered, softly, "or is there a city guard watching us from the alleyway behind me?" She squeezed my arms. "Be discreet, I would not want to spook him."

A furtive glance in the indicated direction revealed a shadowy figure leaning against the side of a building, his uniform mostly hidden beneath an unseasonal cloak that made him stand out worse than if he had not bothered. I ducked my chin and leaned in as if to smell the Amazon's hair.

"There is. And there should be another one around here, somewhere. They followed us from the bazaar."

Kissa nodded. "I noticed that, too, though I only saw the one."

"They took turns so they would not risk losing or alerting us. The uniform is the same, and they are of similar builds, but one wears his sword on the other hip."

Kissa stepped back and spoke through a forced smile. "What do you think they want?"

"I am more concerned by who they work for," I admitted. "Kissa, there is something you should know. It is about the Arch—"

Before I could say more, a rock soared past us and struck the side of Mustafa's shop. Kissa and I spun as one to find the merchant's freckled nephew waving frantically at us from an alleyway further down the street. Kissa and I exchanged startled looks.

"What is it you think he wants?" I asked.

"Perhaps Mustafa sent him?" Kissa shrugged. "There is only one way to know for sure."

"And if it's a trap?"

"Then we will spring it."

"Of course we will," I replied, amused by the utter certainty in her voice. "After you, then?"

"*Dankeschön.*"

The boy met us at the mouth of the alley, his face hidden once more beneath the scarf around his neck. He gestured for us to follow, leading us farther into the shadows before speaking.

"I know where to find the Signora you are looking for," he said.

Kissa and I exchanged looks.

"Did Mustafa send you?" she asked.

"No, my Uncle does not know I am speaking with you. This is my secret to sell, not his."

"I see." Kissa put her hands on both hips. "And why should we believe you?"

"Why would I lie? I overhear you speaking to Uncle. You wish to see the Signora. I can help."

"Help how? We already know where she is."

"Yes, but I think you do not know how to get past the guards. This I have done." The child tapped his chest repeatedly. "I have found a passage no one else knows about."

"Really?" I asked, struck by the boy's suspiciously serendipitous offer. "And you are certain your Uncle did not put you up to this?"

The boy shook his head so adamantly he had to adjust his cap to keep it from falling off. "Uncle would kill me if he found out I had gone down into the cisterns. He says the tunnels are dangerous. Besides, I cannot show him the way. He would sell the route to the highest bidder, and I would get nothing."

"And what is it you want?" Kissa asked.

"I wish to become a Purifier." The boy puffed up his chest. "For this, I will show you the way. But you must swear to take me with you when you leave."

"You want what, now?" I asked, surprised.

"To become a Purifier. Like you."

"Why?"

"Because I am sick of this place," the boy replied, sniffing disdainfully. "I want to learn how to fight monsters and kill people I do not like. I want to go on adventures."

"And what about your mother?" Kissa asked. "Surely she would be sad to see you go."

"This is best for us, both. She does not treat me like a man. I will go, and she will see I do not need her to take care of me. When I return, she will be proud."

"I do not think she would agree with that," Kissa said.

"It doesn't matter," I interjected. "We cannot risk taking him with us. Nero would have my head."

"Please, I will do whatever you ask!"

"I am sorry, lad, but the truth is you are too old. Even if I agreed to your terms, the Order would not accept you."

"They would not make an exception?"

"Once, perhaps. But times have changed. They no longer allow it."

The boy slumped, crestfallen.

"But," I went on, "if you are still willing to show us how to reach this Signora of the Cisterns, I would be willing to pay you."

"With what?"

"With this." I fetched a silver deni from my purse and held it up for him to see. His eyes widened, jaw dropping. It seemed that, even accounting for inflation, a whole silver was still enough to capture a boy's attention. "I will give you one now, and another when the job is done. Do we have a deal?"

"I want ten silvers."

"Ten?!"

The boy nodded.

"You must be—"

"We will pay your price," Kissa interjected, nudging me. "You have our word. But first, we need to lose a couple city guards. Can you help us with that?"

The child grinned.

VII

WHAT LIES BELOW

The boy's name was Ahmet. He was born on the eastern shores of the Golden Horn where his mother had worked for many years as a housekeeper in the home of a senator until her employer cast both her and her newborn baby out for fear his wife would see her husband's features reflected in the infant's face. In this, the senator's hunch had proven correct, for Ahmet, though darker complected, looked a great deal like his father—himself a nobleman from northern Italia.

"Or so my mother tells me," Ahmet continued. "He and I have never met, and she does not speak much of him for fear I will seek him out. She knows I plan to find and kill him for what he has done to us."

From behind, the boy was a slender, skulking shadow, barely discernible against the blackness of the subterranean tunnel we crept through. He raised the candle I had given him to guide our way with open reverence, and its flickering light chased away the gloom for the briefest of moments, illuminating a branch in the tunnels. Ahmet cupped his hand around its dancing flame and took the path to the right—our third, by my count.

"We live in Wallings, now," he went on. "My mother works in the southern market selling carpets for a drunk. It is better than working waterside, but it does not pay enough. That is why I started to steal, until Uncle caught me. Now, I steal for him. Mother does not like it, but I can tell she is relieved that Uncle has gotten involved."

"Poor child," Kissa muttered under her breath.

I nodded. Ahmet's was not a particularly pleasant tale, though hardly unique in a city as obsessed with class and status as Constantinople. Here, the wealthy fed off the weak, rising to positions of power by climbing preordained ladders. Children like Ahmet and women like his mother—they were the rungs.

"But now Uncle has Faruq, who is bad at many things and dumb as ghoul shit, but already a better thief than I will ever be. Soon, Uncle will have no use for me."

Kissa barked a laugh, surprising us both. "I have known your uncle for many years, Ahmet. He can find a use for anything, or anyone. It is his greatest talent, and one of his very few redeeming qualities."

"Then why does he not teach me as he teaches Faruq?" Ahmet asked, turning.

"Perhaps Faruq needs more lessons than you do to stay alive. Or perhaps your uncle needs Faruq to be good at other things. You strike me as a clever boy. Perhaps too clever for your own good. If I were your uncle, I would be wary what I taught you for fear you would get yourself into trouble."

Ahmet hung his head, looking embarrassed. "He has said this to me."

"Perhaps you should listen."

"I will try," he replied, brightening. "Come, it is not far, now."

"How can he tell?" Kissa whispered to me once the boy was a tad farther ahead. "Everything looks the same down here."

I cast a look over one shoulder but could see nothing moving in the darkness. The guards were, of course, long gone; Ahmet had led us through a maze of streets until not even we knew where we were. Still, I could not shake the feeling we were being watched.

The Amazon paced next to me in ankle-deep water, her feet bare, boots in hand, while I padded awkwardly through the muck. My own gait was thrown by the bulky satchel slung across my hip—retrieved from the ruck-sack I left behind in an alcove at the entrance to the tunnels.

"Maybe he is lost and not telling us," I ventured, helpfully.

"You are not funny."

"Who said I was trying to be funny?"

I hastened after the boy before the Amazon could reply, sweat prickling my brow despite the damp chill that pervaded these tunnels. The heavy leather overcoat I wore was to blame for most of it, admittedly, but the rest was pure nervousness; I never had cared for cramped, sunless spaces and their inevitable surplus of dead ends, rotting corpses, and diseased water.

"Here it is," Ahmet said as we turned a corner to stand before what appeared to be one of those dreaded dead ends.

"Well, that settles it." I patted Kissa's shoulder. "We are all going to die down here."

Kissa shrugged me off. "Ahmet, what do you mean? This is a wall."

"No, it is a door." Ahmet raised the candle and pointed to parallel veins of white quartz that ran up the wall. "These are the seams. And the handle is...here."

While Kissa and I stood staring, Ahmet thrust his against what I had mistaken for an occlusion in the stone and pushed. A deafening clang rang out as though some mechanism beyond the wall had been disengaged, followed immediately by a hiss of steam and a series of clanks. Green light —brighter by far than the faint illumination our eyes had grown used to— poured from those parallel seams, framing the door Ahmet had insisted was there all along.

"There," he said. "Now, all you have to do is push on either side. It spins. See?"

Ahmet pushed lightly, and the door revolved to reveal a narrow walkway lined with ventlight sconces. Kissa and I shielded our eyes, though in that sudden strobe of light I saw reflected in her face the same wonder and confusion I felt at discovering something so marvelous in so unlikely a location.

"Ahmet," I said, "how did you know about this place? I don't see how you could have stumbled upon it on your own. Who taught you how to work this contraption?"

"It was the Signora. She showed me what to do. She said it was foolish to keep sneaking past the guards."

"How often do you come to see her?"

"Many times. She has no one to talk to, so I visit when I can. You are lucky. The floor is lit, which means she is alone and wants to talk."

"And if it was unlit?"

"Then it means the guards are below, or that the Praetor is here. She works for him, you see. He comes to ask her questions."

"Questions like what? What could the Praetor need to know about history that he couldn't find out from one of his advisors?"

"He does not ask the Signora about the past. He asks about the future. She does not like it, but she has no choice."

"Ahmet," I began, then paused. "Is the Signora dangerous?"

"Dangerous?"

"Will she call the guards when she sees it is not just you who has come? Or maybe attack us, somehow?"

Ahmet shook his head. "She is strange, but she would not hurt anyone."

"How is she strange?" Kissa asked, helpfully.

Ahmet paused to think about it for a moment. "She does not always make sense. Not like the droolers that hang around Gateside, but like she is talking to someone who is not there."

"Great," I muttered.

Kissa and I exchanged looks, but I did not have to see her face to know what we were both thinking: we had come too far to retreat, now. Addled or not, there was a chance this Signora of the Cisterns held the key to lifting an ancient curse and saving people's lives. And, for that, we had to be willing to take a risk—even if that meant consulting a raving lunatic locked away in the bowels of a metropolis on the orders of the second most powerful man in an Empire that spanned continents.

"I'm going to go in, first," I said, drawing Kissa aside. "Once I'm certain no one is lying in wait on the other side, I will call for you and the boy. Until then, stay out here and be prepared to run."

"You think it may be a trap?"

"I don't know what to think," I admitted. "I cannot imagine why Otho would keep some poor woman sequestered in the cisterns below the city under constant guard. It makes no sense."

"She could be a mistress, perhaps."

I grunted. "It would be a very odd place to keep one, but I suppose it's possible. Either way, I think it best to risk as little as we must. If something happens, write to Nero and tell him everything that has happened since we left. And pass on that tidbit about the Cappadocian priesthood. He'll want to speak with them."

"Of course, though I do not see why it has to be you. I could just as easily go."

"You could, but then I would probably owe you yet another drink, and I am already short on coin as it is. Speaking of which...Ahmet! Blow out that candle until I get back. If someone catches you holding it while I am not around, they'll hang you."

"Get back, Signore?"

"Yes. I am going on ahead, just to be safe."

"But the path is lit, Signore."

"I know that. And I have no doubt you are right to think your friend is alone. But I would never have survived this long were I not exceedingly cautious. Now, the candle."

"Yes, Signore." Ahmet wore a forlorn expression as he stared down at the writhing flame, but eventually blew it out.

"Good lad."

Kissa squeezed my arm. "Be careful."

"I will. I should not be long. If I have not returned in ten minutes time, assume I was captured, and retreat to the surface."

"I do not take orders from you," the Amazon replied with a wry smile, releasing my arm. "I will wait as long as I wish."

"I suppose I deserved that."

In reply, Kissa planted a kiss on my cheek and stepped away. As I turned to go, I felt a tug on my sleeve and looked back to find Ahmet standing not a few feet away with his eyes averted.

"What is it, lad?"

"When you first enter the cistern, be careful where you step. There are a set of stairs, and you could fall if you are not careful."

I patted the boy's shoulder. "Thank you. And do not worry, this is merely me being thorough. I am sure all will be as you have said. Listen for my call."

With that, I reached out to push against the rotating door. It gave way slowly, accompanied by the groan of grinding stone, until at last I was able to slip through and step into that narrow corridor—forced to turn sideways to avoid grazing my shoulders on the walls. The fit was so tight, in fact, that I found myself wondering for what purpose this secret passage had originally been built.

I was still mulling over the mystery when I reached the door at the end of the passageway. The thing was made entirely of copper, albeit coated in a patina of rust so thick that it might as well have been carved from jade, and

219

had a solid iron ring for a handle. The metal hinges groaned as I tugged, inching open with every pull. I gritted my teeth and dug in my heels, yanking on the bloody thing until at last it swung open with a resounding, cacophonous clang that could have woken the dead.

VIII

PROPHECY

*A*fter causing such a ruckus, I fully expected to find a dozen men with pistols drawn waiting on the other side of the doorway. Instead, I found myself alone on a landing connecting a dimly lit flight of steps headed in opposite directions. Indeed, there was no sign of the Signora, or anyone else for that matter; but for the sound of the heavy copper door creaking shut behind me, all was silent and still. I hastily removed my satchel and used it to prop the thing open. Once assured it would hold, I went searching for a better vantage point from which to take stock of my surroundings.

Even from a dais at the top of the stairs, I could see but a fraction of the enormous, subterranean chamber. Indeed, I had to squint to spot the entrance some hundred yards away, all but hidden beyond rows of imposing columns which stood like trees in a orchard—their trunks drenched in knee-deep water that reflected the iridescent light of the dozens of ventlamps ensconced upon the walls, their tops branching into an array of masterfully carved arches that blanketed the ceiling like the cloisters of a cathedral.

Relieved to find the underground reservoir as deserted as Ahmet claimed it would be, I was moments from returning to the others when I noticed ripples disturbing the otherwise placid surface of the water below. Waves lapped against stone as a figure wrapped in a dark cloak and mourner's shawl waded out from the darkened recesses at the furthest edge of the pool. A sibilant voice slithered through the room, its warble like that of two women speaking in tandem.

Who is that upon the stairs, smelling of bones and catacombs?

Unsettled by the unusual cadence of that eerie rhyme, I said nothing. Instead, I crouched down beside the railing, peeking through the bars as that shrouded figure drifted forward, not wading so much as gliding, through the water to stand before the base of a column unlike the others— its stone face that of a Gorgon with snakes for hair, her eyes pupiless and staring, lips curled in a knowing smile.

So it is you, son of none. We have been waiting. Speak, for we would hear the voice of one so long awaited.

"Are you the Signora of the Cisterns?" I asked, emboldened. "I am a friend of Ahmet's."

Friend? You need not stretch the truth. We know already why you have come, even if you do not.

"Somehow I doubt that," I replied, though I could not shrug off the sense that something was very wrong, here—that I had made an egregious error in judgment by stepping foot in this place.

You doubt many things, son of none. But that does not matter. Your path was always going to lead you here, one day. Come into the light so we may see you better.

I rose, revealing myself.

Better. Now, it is our turn.

So slowly it was almost painful to watch, the Signora drew back her shawl. Beneath lay the delicate, unfinished face of a girl perhaps half my age —a budding beauty spoiled by eyes which glowed neon green, their obscene colour blazing as bright as any ventlamp. Hers were the eyes of the tainted, the Devil-touched—those whose very souls have been corrupted by the consumption of the ore our world depends on.

"You are an infernal," I whispered, my heart pounding in my chest. "A witch."

Wrong. Witches are made. We were born. For centuries, they have called us oracles. Prophetesses. Seers. We are the Pythia, and we are your salvation.

I shook my head. "That's impossible. All the oracles were wiped out long before the Order was even founded."

Our power was too much like that of the gods, meant to be believed in but never seen with one's own eyes. So we hid. We practiced our religion, kept our traditions, and waited.

"Waited for what?"

To be found.

"This was a mistake," I muttered, backing away from the railing. "I should never have come down here."

The time for that has passed, son of none. You must listen to what we have to say, for fate itself has brought you here.

"No, I refuse!" I pinned my hands over my ears. "Every word comes out of your lips is a lie. That is always your kind's game, no matter what you call yourself. You are tricksters. Deceivers."

You give us too much credit. We are what we are—as much of this world as any stone or brook or sea.

Though I tried to ignore her, I could not drown out the sound of her voice in my head.

Mankind exists in a thunderstorm, unable to see past the rain, and yet you blame us as one might fault the lightning. But you know this already. You saw it in the face of a starving ghoul. You were meat to her. Nothing more.

"Enough."

There is no need to deceive the blind.

"I said that's enough!"

We do not chastise. We but hold the mirror. Now, let us part the heavens so that you may decide what to do with all that you have been given, as every man one day must.

"What does that even mean?"

As if in answer, light began to play along the girl's exposed skin—flashes of emerald surging across her face like sunlight piercing through clouds. The oracle flung out both arms as more light began pouring out of her gaping mouth. Words soon followed, bursting from her lips in an eardrum-bursting wail that seemed to burn itself indelibly into my brain.

Misfortune hounds the son of none, nipping at his shackled heels, for though he knows it not, he who breathes cinders and worships salt is doomed to fail most when he succeeds, and succeed only when he fails. Heed this warning: in the balance between trials and tombs, the scales of the world shall tip, for dead is the head that covets the crown, and not even the richest king may reign while a convict runs free.

With that final word pounding relentlessly into my skull, the oracle collapsed to her knees, her breathing laboured. Feeling sick to my stomach, I reached for the railing only to find my palms slick with blood. When at last I felt well enough to look up, the cistern seemed darker, more sinister than before.

"What in Caesar's name just happened?" I asked, my voice hoarse in my own ears as though I had been the one screaming.

"A prophecy," the oracle said, though this time the voice was that of an exhausted girl's. When she looked up at me, her eyes were an ordinary shade of brown. "One day soon, those words will help you make a choice. A difficult one. But for now, she wants me to warn you. When they come, you must fight. There is no future for us, if you do not."

I opened my mouth to ask any one of the dozens of questions I had been left with, but was immediately interrupted by the sound of clanking metal as three armed guards burst through the entrance and came running down the stairs on the far side of the reservoir.

"Damn!" I cursed.

I was out of time. Worse, it seemed I had gone through all this trouble for nothing. Indeed, there was no way to salvage any of this except to flee while I had the chance—and perhaps flay the boy for sending me into the lion's den without a sword.

I raced down the stairs, hoping to escape into the tunnels before the guards could pick up my trail and follow. Once we were deep enough, I knew there was no way we would be caught. At least not today. The rest would depend on how much the oracle was willing to tell her captors.

Of course, none of that accounted for the copper door being locked shut.

IX

INTERLUDE: THE CULLING

*I*t is odd, the things that stick with you—the tastes and sights and sounds that prick one's memories. How the sight of blood, the sound of hurried footsteps from behind, or the sensation of being trapped can send one into a panic from which there is no respite. I, myself, am haunted by a great many such recollections—though I suppose that is only fair given my tendency to bury them.

The first person I ever killed out of malice was a boy of perhaps fifteen, no more than a few months older than me. It was a crisp, cool winter's day in Alexandria, which is to say one could walk about comfortably with neither coat nor shawl. In the dark, underground chamber below the Ludi, dressed in nothing but a loincloth and a leather belt cinched around one's waist, however, I found myself uncomfortably chilly.

"To the arena, *dimachaeri*."

The call came through the door accompanied by Trajan's signature ham-fisted knock. The *doctore* who oversaw the second-years was notorious for moving about like some drunken camel, always banging into things as though unaware just how bulky he really was. Indeed, that was how the man fought, as well—leaning on his opponents until they were too tired to stand before crashing into them with his shield and stabbing at them with his sword.

I rose, wishing I had something to wet my suddenly parched throat, and took hold of my blades. Neither was particularly elegant. Both were short and curved, with flared tips and guards to protect my hands from glancing blows, their blades dulled so as to leave welts instead of gashes. I hefted them, dimly aware that the right felt far more secure in my grip than the left, as it had since I was first tested and given my gladiatorial designation. *Dimachaeri.* The twin blade fighter. The aggressor.

"Ready," I called back in the surest voice I could manage, embracing my role.

The door swung open, and Trajan—a monstrously burly man of dubious age and ethnicity who spoke slowly when he spoke at all—gestured me into the torchlit tunnel that led to the arena. When I moved to walk past, however, Trajan's outstretched arm stayed me.

"Wait," he commanded. "The bout is not yet decided."

I thrust my blades into the sand and rubbed my arms for warmth, annoyed to have been summoned prematurely. "Who's left?"

The *doctore* ignored me, as expected. We were not allowed to know our opponents until we faced them from across the sands. Fortunately, I did not have long to wait; a pitiful wail sounded from beyond the iron gate at the end of the tunnel, chased almost immediately by the jeers of the crowd and the trumpeting of a horn. Trajan spat to one side.

"That will have been Christos, then," I said as I retrieved my blades. I spun them idly, hopping from one foot to the other to improve blood flow. Though taller, I was still a slight child, my muscles underdeveloped compared to those of my peers.

Trajan glanced at me in surprise. "Why would you say that?"

"I recognised the scream. Christos cries in his sleep. They all do." I glanced up at the big man. "Did you bet on him to win? I heard you *doctores* make wagers on us."

Trajan pursed his lips but said nothing.

"What were the odds on me?"

"Long," Trajan growled. "Now, prepare yourself."

"Is it time?" I asked.

"Soon. Wait for the second horn blast."

I did as he suggested, dancing from side-to-side. Trajan no doubt thought me anxious, but in that he would have been mistaken. I was not nervous, but eager. Eager to put an end to their petty, underhanded games

—to break someone like I had been broken. And for that, this contest was my best and, possibly, only chance.

They called it the Culling.

Every year from age twelve until we turned eighteen, we initiates were pitted against one another in the arena. Today was not about progress or aptitude, but about separating those who had what it took to survive, and those who did not. Indeed, the Culling was founded on the simplest of principles: the victorious rose and the vanquished fell.

The fallen were given no choice but to leave the Order, sent away to apprentice in some menial trade befitting their ancillary skills. Sadly, the longer one remained, the harder that transition proved; by their late teens, few of us were suited to everyday life. Indeed, those who did not kill themselves routinely became soldiers for hire.

The second horn blew.

"To war," Trajan said, saluting me.

"To war."

I stepped out onto the sands and blinked against the bright sunlight. Gathered round in the stands were those initiates of the other classes, seated according to rank and status, their numbers dwindling in direct proportion to their age. Some I knew, others I did not, though all but the youngest glared at me—resenting me for being considered years later than was proper, after so many of their friends had already been cast out. And they were not the only ones; the *doctores*, sitting apart from the rest, broke with decorum and spoke amongst themselves as I was announced.

"The *dimachaeri!*"

The crowd was silent but for a few claps from the High Council's table and those first years who did not yet know better.

"And his challenger," the herald continued, raising his other hand. "The scissor!"

On the other side of the arena, a tall, lanky boy came striding forth with both hands raised in triumph. The crowd cheered, many of them gesturing to his signature weapon with looks of jealousy and admiration. The scissor—a metal casing that ran from forearm to fist and ended with a crescent-shaped blade—glinted in the sunlight. In the boy's dominant hand, he held a short, stubby sword known as a gladius.

The boy himself was named Dante. He was from Italia, trained to fight from his youth by an uncle who had served as a high-ranking officer in the

Imperial army, and therefore the closest thing to a noble the Order would ever recruit.

He was also my greatest tormentor.

"Let the bout begin!"

I went after him like a rabid dog. Heedless of my own safety, I closed the distance between us in a full sprint that caught Dante flat-footed. He raised his weapons as if to block and parry, but I was not interested in playing by the stagnant rules drilled into us by the *doctores*. I was not here merely to win, but to prove I belonged—that I was not only better, but more worthy.

The crowd gasped as I threw my offhand blade like a javelin, launching it midstride. Dante ducked, allowing the weapon to sail harmlessly overhead. Which was exactly what I had hoped he would do—the instant he crouched, I used every bit of momentum to ram my knee into his face. He reeled backwards, nose shattered, but did not fall. Instead, he dropped his own sword and tried to blindly tackle me to the ground.

As he hooked his sword arm around my waist, I thought about those nightly slaps to keep me from a good night's sleep. My clothes stolen or dunked in urine. The lies that sent me to the wrong lesson at the wrong time. The infliction of pain when no one was looking. And how, until now, I had been unable to do anything for fear of disobeying the Order's strict policy on unsanctioned violence. But not today. Today, I was free to show them all what I was capable of when pushed too far for far too long. Today, they were all going to see why I had been chosen.

I twisted as we fell, wrapped both hands around the metal tube encasing his arm, and used Dante's own momentum to drive the dull tip of his crescent-shaped blade up into the soft tissue behind his chin the instant we hit the sand. It pierced the skin and embedded itself through the roof of his mouth. He began gagging on his own blood, his eyes impossibly wide as he slowly slumped to one side. I sat up, watched the life drain from his face, and felt nothing but the grim satisfaction of having done what had to be done.

X

FAREWELLS

Once I realised the door would not budge, I began banging on it, slamming a balled fist against the metal until I thought it might break. My satchel, inexplicably, lay at my feet. Behind me, the three members of the Praetorian guard—soldiers dressed like legionnaires from a bygone era under the command of Otho, himself—had reached the oracle and were escorting her to the other end of the cistern. They would be coming for me, next.

"Kissa! Ahmet! Open the door!"

I stopped knocking, alerted by the sound of a woman's voice calling to me from the other side. I thrust my ear against the corroded metal.

"Kissa?"

"Valentine! Is that you?"

"Yes! Hurry and open the door! The guards found me and will be here, soon. We need to run!"

"I cannot! Ahmet must have done something to the door. I cannot get it to open!"

"Where's Ahmet? Have him fix it!"

"When the sconces went out, he ran back into the tunnels with the candle and left me here! I can hardly see my hand in front of my face. Valentine...I will not be able to make it back to the surface."

I cursed, realising too late how much trust we placed in the boy. Still, he had seemed so sincere, and why flee without getting his coin? Was it fear, perhaps? And why had he neglected to mention what the oracle was? Even a child knew how to recognise one of the Devil-touched. Unfortunately, there was no time to dwell on any of that, not if we hoped to survive.

"Kissa, listen to me!" I insisted. "Put your back to the door, walk until you reach the door in the wall, then turn right. Find the left wall, then take your first left. Then two rights. A second left. And two more rights. Repeat it back to me."

"Right, left, two rights, left, two rights."

"Good. By then, you should be under the grates and able to see. From there, follow the sound of music. There was a street performer playing not far from where we snuck into the tunnels."

"What if there is no performer, or he has moved?"

"Then follow the smell of the candle. It's scented. Rosemary, I think. Either way, you should be able to find a way out."

"And what about you?"

"Don't worry about me. There are only three of them, and I have my gear with me. I've faced worse odds."

"And won, right? You are supposed to say you have faced worse odds and won!"

"Does surviving count?" I asked. A glance over my shoulder revealed one of the men standing guard over the oracle at the base of the stairs while the other two waded towards me brandishing a blade and a spear, respectively. "Go, now! I will come find you as soon as I can."

"Find me where?"

"Right. There is a tavern on the waterfront with a blue crab on its sign. I know the owner. Tell her who you are, and that Valentine sent you. She'll sort you out until I get there."

"The waterfront? Why there?"

"Because the owner has a physician on retainer, and I have a feeling I'm going to need one when I make it out of here."

"*Scheisse.*" Kissa groaned in frustration and slammed a hand against the door.

"Listen, Kissa. Whatever happens, I will endure it better knowing you are safe."

There was a long pause. "Very well, but if you are not there by tomorrow afternoon, I am going to come looking for you."

"Hopefully it won't come to that. Now, go! And, if you happen to catch up to Ahmet, be sure to wring his scrawny neck for me, will you? And take back that candle. It was a gift."

Kissa barked a laugh. "Good luck, Valentine. I will see you soon."

"Count on it."

I slapped the door with the flat of my palm before grabbing my satchel and bolting for the stairs; I could not risk a pitched battle with such poor footing. Instead, I returned to the dais. From there, I could see the two guards racing up the stairs.

For a moment, I considered surrender. I was a Purifier, after all. In an ideal world, I could claim a rumour had brought me down here to deal with an infernal. Legally, I would have every right to do so, if not for the irrefutable fact that the oracle was being guarded by the Praetor's own men.

Whether his intent was to shelter the infernal or hold her against her will, the law was clear: she was an abomination, and harbouring her kind was tantamount to a death sentence. Even Otho could not be seen flouting that provision, which meant he could not risk leaving anyone who had spoken to the oracle alive.

Especially not someone like me.

With a curse, I dumped the contents of my satchel on the floor and retrieved those few items I could rely on to deal with flesh and blood enemies. Still, I was fortunate to find myself prepared by the time the two men finally ascended the stairs.

"Hold, this is all a mis—" I began, hoping they might drop their guard if I pleaded with them, first.

It did not work.

Instead, the soldier with the blade lunged forward, hacking at me like I was some common thief he could dispatch with a casual strike. I hastily raised the scissor I had earned many years after killing Dante and deflected the stroke. Then, with a move I had practiced so many times it felt as natural as breathing, I slid past my assailant and ran my offhand blade along his thigh—leaving behind a superficial wound meant to discourage rather than to dispatch.

The soldier cursed and hobbled off clutching at his leg while his companion came in low, lunging with a spear that nicked my shoulder even as I spun and chopped at his spear with my gladius. The shaft did not sever as I had hoped, but it did draw the soldier off balance enough that a swift kick to his ornamental chest plate sent him sprawling.

I turned, hoping to find the path to the stairs unobstructed. If I could reach them, I might be able to rush to the exit and escape. I doubted the third guard would try to stop me; keeping the oracle safe was clearly his main priority.

Before I could so much as take a step, however, a sword stroke fell across my back, landing with enough force to drive me to my knees. Fortunately, the leather of my coat—not to mention the metal plates sewn into it— protected me from a much nastier wound. Unfortunately, the next one could just as easily take my head off.

Rather than risk it, I whirled and threw myself at the nearest soldier, throwing every ounce of weight into a leaping tackle that must have taken us both over the railing because suddenly we were plunging towards the water headfirst. Though it must have taken seconds at most, I remember it felt like an agonisingly long drop to the bottom.

In an unbelievable stroke of luck, I landed on top of the guard and bounced off his chest plate, the wind knocked out of my lungs seconds before reservoir water came rushing into my mouth. I managed to roll to one side and stayed there, too stunned to move. Overhead, the soldier with the spear was leaning over the edge to look down at us.

I must have looked terrible. Dripping wet and likely bleeding internally, I had lost my gladius in the fall, though I still wore the scissor—another miracle, given how easily I could have impaled myself upon it.

The guard I had used to break my fall looked even worse. He lay propped against the base of a column, his breathing shallow, a shard of bone poked out from beneath his greaves. A man with an injury like that would walk with a limp for the rest of his life. Which, in his case, was not long.

Let him die at his own pace, son of none. You have done your part. Allow them to arrest you.

The words rang throughout the cistern. I managed to sit up and saw the oracle standing between myself and the third guard with her palms raised as though imploring us all to stop the fighting. But it was too late for that. I knew I was too hurt to escape this place on foot, just as I knew these men were not interested in arresting me. If they had been, they would have asked me to surrender from the start. Besides, I had hurt one of their own.

This was only going to end one way.

Climbing to my feet was agony, but I managed it. Walking proved tougher, but I managed that, too. To my left, I could hear the guard with the spear descending the stairs, his greaves clinking with every footfall. I would have to take care of him, next.

It is enough, son of none. Rest, now. Do not—

I ignored her and punched down with the scissor—a savage blow that drove the crescent-shaped blade into the wounded guard's exposed throat. It bit deep, tearing through flesh and bone. Blood spurted from the gaping wound and pooled around his head, darkening the already murky waters even as I yanked the blade free with a wet gurgle.

Fool, look what you have done!

I turned to find the oracle and her guard staring, not at me, but at the water on the far end of the cistern where strange beasts swam beneath the surface, disturbing it like sharks swarming to the scent of blood.

Panicked, I stumbled backwards until I ran into a column, watching as shapes began to rise from the water—faceless, limbless creatures emerging like shrouded figures that had been stretched almost impossibly thin, they continued to grow until each stood taller than a man, the water drawn tight over their eerie silhouettes while every ventlamp in sight went out, one by one, their light sucked into the very core of these foul, faintly glowing infernals.

"What are they?" the guard with the spear asked as he reached the bottom of the stairs and flattened himself against the nearest wall, clearly terrified.

The Ardow. The souls of the drowned.

I balked at the name. I had heard of the Ardow, of course, but they were known to require the deaths of dozens, if not hundreds, to manifest. You might find one lurking about a sunken ship or in a collapsed cave, but never so many as this.

"Where did they all come from?" I asked, fighting against the urge to turn and run as the menacing creatures began slinking towards us.

This is where the water ends.

"Of course," I replied, reminded of the corpses known to line the water-side docks most mornings. "Why are they here?"

You summoned them when you killed the man who would have drowned. You took from them, and now they will take from you.

As if on cue, the Ardow surged forward, leaping onto the guard with the spear one at a time, like flying fish. The soldier struggled to fend them off, but it was as if he were trapped beneath a waterfall, his every scream cut short until he lay face down in the water, bobbing gently.

The Ardow swiftly retreated, their emerald green hearts pulsing with enough light to show the guard had gotten pulled onto his side in their wake. Half his face was submerged, and his lone, bulging eye stared at me in horror like some dreadful accusation.

Before I could so much as call out, the Ardow surged forward once more, only this time towards me. Though I knew it was useless to do so, I raised my scissor. Unfortunately, the Ardow were essentially spirits, and spirits could not be cut. Indeed, trying to harm them physically was like attempting to blow out a wildfire—utterly pointless. Indeed, everything I might have used to fend them off was at the top of a winding set of stairs I could never hope to reach in time.

Resolved to run towards the exit instead, I broke away from the column, only to stumble as something grazed my thigh and sent fresh pain lancing across it. I looked down and found blood staining yet another ruined pair of trousers. I fell against the column, dimly aware that I had been shot.

At that exact moment, a wave hit me from behind and sent me sprawling. Another crashed in from my left, then my right, and my left again. I sputtered, trying to catch my breath, but the waves were hitting me too fast. I gagged and spat, my nostrils flooded, my eyes stinging. Everything started to go black until another wave, this one somehow more powerful than the last, slammed me so hard against the column I felt something in me shatter.

The sudden burst of pain brought me back to consciousness in the worst imaginable way. Indeed, as the barrage continued, I found myself thinking about what Nero told that sailor so long ago—his horrifying tale of being dragged behind a ship for hours and hours until at last you simply succumbed to exhaustion and wished for death.

I was not going to last hours.

I do not remember much of what happened next. I remember a brilliant flash of green light and the strangely guttural groans of men and women screaming underwater. I remember two faces hovering above my own. The first, that of a girl with glowing neon eyes. The other a stranger's, and yet so much more familiar, for his was a visage I had seen on every silver deni I had ever held—including the very first that had gotten me into this mess to begin with.

High Praetor Otho, a man second only to the Emperor himself.
Oh, yes, and he held a blade to my throat.
Let us not forget that.

XI

POSTSCRIPT

*T*he *carcer* is quiet, now, the hallway beyond the bars dark and deserted—almost as though the priests who paid my jailers a visit in the early hours of the morning were never here, at all.

It was the sound of their slippered feet that woke me. My jailers wear sandals, you see, the slap of their steps completely distinct from the hissing tread of holy men. Of course, their voices would have done so, eventually; from the moment they arrived wrapped in their dark cloaks and pale-yellow kaftans that distinguish their sect, the terra-cotta priests spoke loudly in Greek.

Worried they might be harbingers of further trouble, I slipped out from beneath the single sheet I had been given and hid my cache of letters—including my most recent featuring my first meeting with the oracle known as the Pythia and my capture at the hands of the Praetor. Then, as furtively as I had crawled out of it, I returned to my bed, content to watch through slitted eyes while feigning sleep. That was until a familiar, albeit altogether unexpected, voice drifted through the narrow crack in the wall beside my head.

"They talk of you, dead man."

I stiffened, startled as much by the speaker's use of my native tongue as the words themselves.

"They come to scold our minders," my neighbour continued. "They say you must not be left alone. They say you are *sicarius*...I do not know this word."

"Assassin," I replied, sensing there was little to be gained by staying silent. "It means assassin."

"Really? Whom did you kill? Wait, do not answer. I do not want to know." My neighbour fell silent for a moment. "Now they say you are *emissarius*. A spy. This word I know. They wish to see what you write. They say they will find hidden messages in your words. This is why they give you parchment."

I grunted, slightly tickled at the thought of what anyone other than a member of the Order would make of my seemingly illegible scribbles.

"They speak now of the world outside," he continued. "There is a local sickness. Many have fallen ill. They complain about this and other things."

My neighbour fell silent as the priests and guards droned on, the exchange more a conversation now than a dressing down. Still, I craned my ears, hoping to hear something of current events. I had almost given up, however, when I caught a familiar name tucked away amidst their inane chatter. Indeed, several familiar names.

"They just mentioned a man's name," I hissed, rapping lightly against the wall with my knuckles. "Nero. And there was something about the Habsburgs. What was it? What did they say?"

There was no answer.

"Please, I need to know what they are saying."

"You need nothing," my neighbour snapped. "A dead man has no needs. You will find this out soon enough."

I decided to change tactics. "And would you deny a man his dying wish? All I ask is that you tell me what they were talking about."

"War, dead man," he replied after a lengthy pause. "They speak of a holy war."

Hours have passed since he spoke those words, and no matter how many times I ask nor how many pleas I make, he refuses to answer. It seems I am to be left with nothing but wild speculation and useless conjecture. Could this so-called holy war have something to do with me? What could the Cappadocian priests possibly hope to find in my letters? Does this mean none of what I write will be sent to Alexandria?

I have no answers. Worse, this news has revealed an inconvenient truth: despite my resignation to the possibility, I do not wish to die here. Indeed, penning these pages has reminded me what it is like to live outside a prison cell—what it is to want to live. Sadly, this epiphany changes nothing. I have done all I can. All that is left for me now is to continue my tale and pray these letters reach those who can make sense of them before it is too late.

With regards,
A Not Yet Dead Man

To Be Continued...

ACKNOWLEDGMENTS

First and foremost, I would like to thank Argento Publishing for taking on this book—and, by extension, me. To my rockstars on the Alpha Team, know that your invaluable feedback was instrumental in making this book what it has become. To my wonderful ARC readers, I cannot tell you how thankful I am for your thoughts and support. To Lane Hamilton, thank you for being the rock I needed to see this thing through to the end. To my brilliant editor, thank you for your wonderful suggestions and seemingly infinite patience—I never would have been able to do this without you in my corner. To Ben Kerr, thank you for putting together such a magnificent cover and all the other integral work you have done to improve the aesthetics of this book. To Shayne Silvers, thank you for literally everything else. Our partnership and your consistent mentorship has genuinely changed my life for the best. And, of course, to the love of my life, Alexandra: thank you for encouraging me as I strove to put out the best product I possibly could no matter how many deadlines I overshot or how many tireless hours I spent toiling away when we could have been swimming with sea turtles. Without your constant support, this book would not have been even half as good as it is. You are incredible beyond words, and I am so glad that I get to share in this success with you.

ABOUT THE AUTHOR

Cameron O'Connell was born in Berlin, Germany, in 1989 and lives in Washington, DC with his wife. A former model, soldier, and teacher, Cameron writes the Echoes of Ventlight volumes and is a co-author of the Amazon Bestselling Phantom Queen Diaries.

MAKE A DIFFERENCE

Reviews are the most powerful tools in my arsenal when it comes to getting attention for my books. Much as I'd like to, I don't have the financial muscle of a New York publisher.

But I do have something much more powerful and effective than that, and it's something that those publishers would kill to get their hands on.

A committed and loyal bunch of readers.

Honest reviews of my books help bring them to the attention of other readers.

If you've enjoyed this book, I would be very grateful if you could spend just five minutes leaving a review on my book's Amazon page.

Thank you very much in advance.

TRY: WHISKEY GINGER (PHANTOM QUEEN DIARIES # 1)

*T*he pasty guitarist hunched forward, thrust a rolled-up wad of paper deep into one nostril, and snorted a line of blood crystals—frozen hemoglobin that I'd smuggled over in a refrigerated canister—with the uncanny grace of a drug addict. He sat back, fangs gleaming, and pawed at his nose. "That's some bodacious shit. Hey, bros," he said, glancing at his fellow band members, "come hit this shit before it melts."

He fetched one of the backstage passes hanging nearby, pried the plastic badge from its lanyard, and used it to split up the crystals, murmuring something in an accent that reminded me of California. Not *the* California, but you know, Cali-foh-nia—the land of beaches, babes, and bros. I retrieved a toothpick from my pocket and punched it through its thin wrapper. "So," I asked no one in particular, "now that ye have the product, who's payin'?"

Another band member stepped out of the shadows to my left, and I don't mean that figuratively, either—the fucker literally stepped out of the shadows. I scowled at him, but hid my surprise, nonchalantly rolling the toothpick from one side of my mouth to the other.

The rest of the band gathered around the dressing room table, following the guitarist's lead by preparing their own snorting utensils—tattered magazine covers, mostly. Typically, you'd do this sort of thing with a dollar-bill, maybe even a Benjamin if you were flush. But fangers like this lot couldn't touch cash directly—in God We Trust and all that. Of course, I didn't really understand why sucking blood the old-fashioned way had suddenly gone out of style. More of a rush, maybe?

"It lasts longer," the vampire next to me explained, catching my mildly curious expression. "It's especially good for shows and stuff. Makes us look, like, less—"

"Creepy?" I offered, my Irish brogue lilting just enough to make it a question.

"Pale," he finished, frowning.

I shrugged. "Listen, I've got places to be," I said, holding out my hand.

"I'm sure you do," he replied, smiling. "Tell you what, why don't you, like, hang around for a bit? Once that wears off," he dipped his head toward the bloody powder smeared across the table's surface, "we may need a pick-me-up." He rested his hand on my arm and our gazes locked.

I blinked, realized what he was trying to pull, and rolled my eyes. His widened in surprise, then shock as I yanked out my toothpick and shoved it through his hand.

"Motherfuck—"

"I want what we agreed on," I declared. "Now. No tricks."

The rest of the band saw what happened and rose faster than I could blink. They circled me, their grins feral...they might have even seemed intimidating if it weren't for the fact that they each had a case of the sniffles —I had to work extra hard not to think about what it felt like to have someone else's blood dripping down my nasal cavity.

I held up a hand.

"Can I ask ye gentlemen a question before we get started?" I asked. "Do ye even *have* what I asked for?"

Two of the band members exchanged looks and shrugged. The guitarist, however, glanced back towards the dressing room, where a brown paper bag sat next to a case full of makeup. He caught me looking and bared his teeth, his fangs stretching until it looked like it would be uncomfortable for him to close his mouth without piercing his own lip.

"Follow-up question," I said, eyeing the vampire I'd stabbed as he gingerly withdrew the toothpick from his hand and flung it across the room with a snarl. "Do ye do each other's make-up? Since, ye know, ye can't use mirrors?"

I was genuinely curious.

The guitarist grunted. "Mike, we have to go on soon."

"Wait a minute. Mike?" I turned to the snarling vampire with a frown. "What happened to *The Vampire Prospero*?" I glanced at the numerous fliers in the dressing room, most of which depicted the band members wading through blood, with Mike in the lead, each one titled *The Vampire Prospero* in *Rocky Horror Picture Show* font. Come to think of it…Mike did look a little like Tim Curry in all that leather and lace.

I was about to comment on the resemblance when Mike spoke up, "Alright, change of plans, bros. We're gonna drain this bitch before the show. We'll look totally—"

"Creepy?" I offered, again.

"Kill her."

Get the full book ONLINE! *http://www.shaynesilvers.com/l/206897*

(Note: Full chronology of all books in the TempleVerse shown on the 'BOOKS BY SHAYNE SILVERS' page.)

ALSO BY CAMERON O'CONNELL

PHANTOM QUEEN DIARIES

(Set in the TempleVerse)

by Cameron O'Connell & Shayne Silvers

COLLINS (Prequel novella #0 in the 'LAST CALL' anthology)

WHISKEY GINGER (BOOK #1)

COSMOPOLITAN (BOOK #2)

OLD FASHIONED (BOOK #3)

MOTHERLUCKER (Novella #2.5 in the 'LAST CALL' anthology)

DARK AND STORMY (BOOK #4)

MOSCOW MULE (BOOK #5)

WITCHES BREW (BOOK #6)

SALTY DOG (BOOK #7)

SEA BREEZE (BOOK #8)

HURRICANE (BOOK #9)

BRIMSTONE KISS (BOOK #10)

MOONSHINE (BOOK #11)

BOOK #12 COMING SOON